Three in a Cage

Front and back cover design
by Luis McCormick
photogenesisajijic@yahoo.com

Book format by Betty Wright
boopmx@gmail.com

Ajijic, Mexico

Jani, Francisco and Max welcome you into
Aztec Art & Weaving Studios

Three in a Cage

A Modest Novel

Janice Kimball

Photography by
Janice Kimball

This book is dedicated to Francisco Urzúa Inés
who has given me the freedom to write
about our life without constraint.

Contents

PREFACE

I bare myself in this book. I have given you, the reader, whatever mystery there ever was about me.

I bare Francisco. He is a man comfortable with who he is. He has led a life as different from other people as mine has been. He has given me permission to tell some of his story as well. I am surprised that Francisco's father, Teo Urzúa, has played such a large a role in this book. I did not originally plan that. I thank Teo for giving me permission to use his real name. He said he would forgive me for whatever I write and that he is glad he does not understand English.

Of course Max Bird does not really speak in human language, but I can imagine what life for him may have been as a purple crested Mexican parrot poached from the wild. I believe Max has a soul. I can see it in his eyes. Sometimes he sits on a stack of books near my computer watching me write and I imagine I am writing what he is telling me, as if in transcription.

I believe it is criminal to buy animals that have been snatched from the wild. Sometimes what we believe and how we feel are two different things. I think Max would have died if I had not bought him. It was a very hot day in Jocotepec and he was an infant hanging onto a stack of bird cages with one foot. I was told he was the last parrot left from that seasons "crop." I emptied my purse. The vendor took all the money I had, and that is how Max Bird joined our family.

The secondary characters in this book are pure fiction. They were constructed from bits and pieces of persons who live around Lake Chapala. There are many Garcías here. Police really do wash their trucks using the gardener's hose on the service drive in front of our place. Francisco, Max and I have watched them from the kitchen balcony. It is not unusual to see people around our lake who use golf carts for transportation, including a woman that drove one with tassels and had a dog ride beside her. The woman in blue linen is a composite of many expatriates I have met. I include these characters to give the flavor of our unique community.

Within the confines of the structure of this book and the confines of our own walls, I have written as true a picture as I can of what goes on in the hearts and minds of those of us who live at Aztec Studios.

Peace, feathers, and enjoy the ride.
Janice

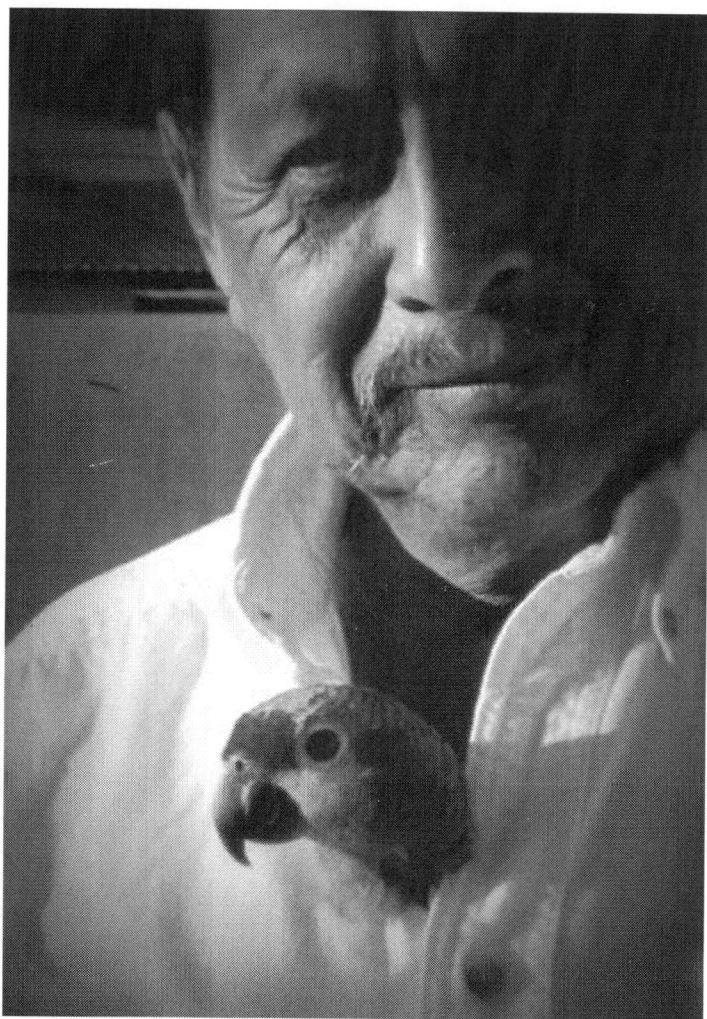

In the beginning, Teo was
Max Bird's whole world.

Three in a Cage

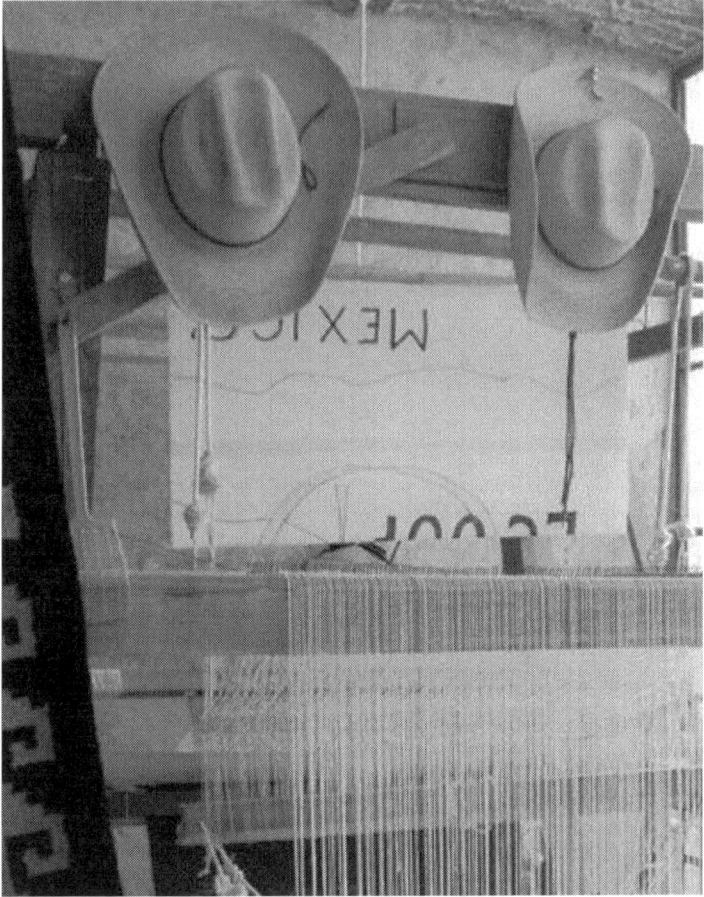

Teo removed his sombrero from the foot
of the ancient loom for the last time.

1
Loss and Adaptation

Teo's straw sombrero had a home with Jani for the last six years. He removed it from the nail at the foot of the ancient loom and placing it on his head left Aztec Studios for good.

"What about Max?" he inquired.

"Max stays here. I bought him and I pay for his birdseed. He is mine," Jani replied.

Brooding clouds drifted among the mountaintops high in Mexico's Sierra Madre where the picturesque village of Ajijic nestled on the shore of Lake Chapala. Their studios were just off the highway west of town. Teo walked toward the bus stop with resolve, yet with halting steps, as Jani looked on with relief and sadness. Teo boarded the bus that would take him back to Jocotepec, the village of his birth, leaving behind his displaced son, Francisco, and Max, the parrot he had nurtured from infancy. He turned before the bus drove off and gave them one backward glance.

Francisco was standing in confusion and wondered if Jani would ask him, like she had asked his father Teo, to find another home. Would she send him back to live in the abandoned silver mine above San Juan Cosalá? Would he again wander in the plaza and sleep in the street? Francisco picked up a pencil from the table and began drawing angels on the wall. It was an act of the hand, not a cognitive gesture, a compulsion sure to anger Jani, but one he could not control.

Voices, nonexistent, screamed at Francisco as he slapped at his ear in an attempt to stop them. "Get out, get out!" they demanded, but he paid them no heed. He wondered if this was the last stop in his 30 years of running, as his legs had become tired, and there was no place else for him to go.

Jani had worked hard to create Aztec Art Studios. It was a beautiful place where Francisco lived with Jani amid colorful paintings of Mexico's indigenous people and racks of tapestries, influenced by the ancients, that Teo had so carefully woven. Sometimes Francisco believed he had been a strand of yarn that had been woven into them as he felt he was part of their existence. When Jani left a ballpoint pen lying around, in a dream state he drew on the walls. He drew doves and angels, he drew them on the television and anything electronic. If a knife was available he tried to carve his initials into his father's loom, but the loom was mesquite, a wood after several centuries was now hard as stone. The loom had spent its youth in the village of Jocotepec, where it had felt that the swaying motion of generations of weavers. It may have originally stood in an adobe structure under a thatched roof beside a family's outdoor kitchen, a baby's hammock strapped to its back. It had witnessed many cycles of life and death and survived to become part of the family that lived at Aztec Studios.

Teo did love Francisco, it cannot be denied. Jani was his mate for five years, and though he did not embody the truth she longed for, he had in his way loved her too. Teo was a master weaver. He wove with fervor to please his woman

2

and demonstrate his prowess. He wove the crocodiles and creatures that lurked on the bottom of Mexico's ancient Lake Texcoco, the mythical gods from ancient scrolls and codices, and he created the long and complex serpents that Jani loved.

Jani drew patterns for Teo's weavings. She liked to watch him as he wove, visualize yet another combination of color, imagine another pattern, and other materials. He loved her to hang out at his loom. It was these times that sustained them. But his diabetes became too advanced for him to continue to weave. Jani begged him to stop, but he kept at it until his pain was so debilitating that he began to hate her for it.

After Teo left, Francisco responded in the only way he knew. He went into the bathroom and pulled out the cans of hair spray Jani had hidden under the sink. He entered the shower and sprayed their contents out the bathroom window. Unlike other times, Jani did not get mad. "I'm taking you to a psychiatrist and having you put on medication," is all she said. She took his hand, and from that time on he believed that he and Jani, along with Max Bird, would face this life together.

Max had been spoiled. He had been able to summon Teo with the feeblest tweet. Teo had nurtured Max beyond what even the very best of mothers would deem reasonable. Max felt it his birthright to be snuggled under Teo's shirt, felt he smelled just like Teo, that chest to chest their hearts beat as one, and that he was Teo's whole world the same as Teo was his. Max never thought beyond this, never noticed the presence of Francisco, and only acknowledged Jani when she came too close to Teo, in which case he would stretch his neck out from under his shirt and bite her. For Max it was a time of bliss, before he knew Teo could walk off

3

without a goodbye, before he had the ability to even conceive that Francisco and Jani would one day crop his flight feathers.

"Max is your responsibility now." Jani told Francisco, who at that time was unable to form words beyond an unintelligible whisper. He could only futilely shake his head back and forth and point at Max, afraid to touch him.

Max had an aura that neither Jani nor Francisco put into words, but both knew. It was a rainbow aura that could be seen when Max tilted his head a certain way, its tertiary colors shimmering as it cast off faint rays with fine intricate endings. On still days, if you were very observant, you could see Max's feathers vibrating, each group to a different set of notes, as if in a silent symphony. Sometimes it seemed to Francisco he could hear music coming from within Max, and words, maybe his and Jani's words. When they were in a room where he was perched, they could feel the warmth of his eyes, curious and filled with wonder, looking at them.

After Teo left, Max began to observe Jani and Francisco in earnest. Scratching at his head he examined first their habits, then feelings, then words and their meanings, thoughts, and motivations. He started forming human words at night in secret. He fantasized about having long legs and arms that he could weave with. He thought that one day he would learn to warble. He dreamed he would do it so well that he would be asked to join a band as the featured singer, but most of all, he dreamed of stopping those bird marketers in Guadalajara's San Juan market from trafficking any more wild birds.

Max had bad days where reality began to surface. Teo had perhaps been his unwilling host. The revelation of that truth flashed before his eyes like infrared light—exposing a truth that lay beneath a simpler plane. In nurturing Max, Teo was

4

insuring his own continued necessity at Aztec Studios and the continuation of his life with Jani, who made life easier for Teo, and for his son as well. Painful confusions and distortions that kept humans from living a straightforward life at first made Max want to keep his distance from them. And he would have, had he not been of a gregarious nature. Often he wished he could go back to being pure bird but he could no longer remember what that felt like. Max did not become aware of the full extent of his metamorphosis for a long time.

The first year the three of them lived together Jani never forgot to give Francisco his medication, although she often forgot to take her own. Each time he thanked her, at first with tears wetting his cheeks. His character took on a strong demeanor, wise and compassionate to the shortcomings of others. Perhaps this trait revealed his Mayan heritage. The medication stilled the skipping neurons that made voices play within, tormenting him with their pleadings and screaming for help.

Max helped Francisco to heal. Each of them was a creature with a beating heart, something to hold, to love; a live being, warm and receptive, to nurture and call their own. They could be seen gazing intently into each other's eyes. Francisco talked to Max quietly for hours in a dialog he felt too insecure to share with other humans. Max always understood and was the keeper of Francisco's secrets, although he himself withheld the words he sometimes wanted to say.

Jani's care of Max and Francisco was not altogether unselfish. They entertained her, freeing her from the desire to seek community outside the shelter of Aztec Studios. She

5

had once dreamed of being an anthropologist, living in a hut in the wilds, discovering how and why humans and animals behaved as they did. Her shelter of Max and Francisco was what she had always wanted for herself but never received. Jani had led her life in an unsafe world. The magic of life now existed for her in subtropical Mexico.

Max recovered from the loss of Teo. He was maturing in a very fine way. His plumage was taking on a fuller and richer coat, his greens more tropical. When he was happy, the violet crest on the top of his head spiked in a distinctive, princely way. The fullness of Max's breast contained the heart of a bird that would have been the leader of a flock had he not merged into the human world of Jani and Francisco.

Max bird loved Jani and Francisco, but he didn't know if he could ever fully adjust to their life. He often wondered why they chose to live in a cage. Especially this strange rectangular cage, much narrower than it was wide, its lookout towering above all the others in the neighborhood as it reached toward the sky. It was up there that he and Francisco sometimes swung in a hammock looking down on the flocks of village people partying and singing in the street. He wondered why Jani and Francisco's hearts didn't skip a beat when cars and trucks filled with people lined up on the highway outside the cage, beeping their horns when Guadalajara's Chivas won a soccer game. He wondered why they didn't have a desire to join the other humans, but he was only a bird and had a lot to learn.

Weaving of a Maya princess in showroom window facing
their cobblestone service drive.

2
Decision to Write

Jani drew an ancient Maya on the large sheet of paper she had rolled out before her; a warrior on parade, his headpiece overpowering his own presence. The real crocodile heads weight was held by a brace that went from the warrior's waist and up the back of his neck, held in position with struts that were supported by the strength of his shoulder muscles. Jani thought about the colors Francisco would use to weave the tapestry that was to be her rendition of what must have been an incredible sight; possibly vivid blues and greens on a maroon background or brilliant purple with canary yellow. "Yes, Jani thought, an ancient Maya weaver would have used one of these combinations of colors had he been present weaving the warrior beside them."

For Jani the motivation behind an art project in the making stemmed from what she had finished before it. Her ideas were generational, one set of creative ideas giving birth to another, which led her to stay in the arena of making interpretations of the pre-Hispanic cultures, perhaps too long. She harbored a secret desire to write, to create on paper of a more modest size, to hold a book of her own making in her hand, one that others would read, be inspired by, learn from, if they chose to create their own world. The book could serve as how-to instructions so that those that tried their style of living would not have to repeat any of their mistakes.

"What are you thinking about, Jani?" Max asked, breaking a long silence.

"I need to write a book," she told him.

"What kind of a book, Jani? Are you going to write about Mexico? Adventure stories? About us at Aztec Studios?" Max Bird chirped from the back of a chair in a voice heard only by the telepathically inclined, as he finished preening a feather.

"I want write about our life together."...'as if we lived in a laboratory,' Jani thought, finding that idea appealing. "I am sure the book *will* be an adventure story, Max, with tales from our very different pasts, of the obstacles we hurdled in our fight to survive, of creating a reality from our lost identities. How could it not be an adventure story? But it could be other things as well. Our studios could also serve as laboratory to discover how to fly without wings.

"You sure want to cover a whole lot of territory in only one book, Jani!" Francisco told her.

"...And why not? Tell me why not, Maestro, why shouldn't she?" Max interjected with a flip of his feathers. Jani was pleased Max asked her what she wanted to write. Sometimes she didn't know if Max was her and Francisco's prodigy or the lead bird in their small flock of a family.

Francisco needed time to reply, as his ideas took on a more definite unchangeable position than those of the others. Jani recognized the depth of his consideration about the path the book should take as he stood beside her as unwavering as a Mesquite, a tree whose roots anchor it through the severest storms. Francisco had a slow but unwavering strength, the fortitude that would enable him to witness a waterspout turn

10

into a mudslide, devastating an entire village, yet also witness the mountains' rebirth, seeds sprouting up from between rocks in the bare earth remaining; the blossoming of new flowers and the return of the butterflies as a metaphor for his own life and its blessings, and feel thankful for what was left. "Yes, Jani thought, Francisco's opinion was very valuable indeed!"

"You could write a book about peace...and love, Jani. Our environment here *could* be a laboratory, and the three of us *could* be used for experiments." Francisco said. "We could prove there are different ways to love, to find peace, and we could share our findings."

"Ohh," Jani said, surprised that Francisco would be so willing to expose their lives. "That sounds like a good idea, Francisco, except I am too old for any more experiences...whoops! I mean experiments!"

"We could become famous!" Francisco said, tugging at his ear.

"But Francisco, maybe you need to think more about this... you know, I have arrived at my future, but you are still contemplating yours...maybe you need to be careful about hanging your laundry out for everyone to see!"

"It's okay, Jani," Francisco said. 'I'm the second oldest of thirteen children, the oldest boy. I never had much attention and I know now that I *like* it!"

"Why don't you write a book with a *lot* of *me* in it?" Max asked, feathers in a big fluff, his hooked bill scraping over his bottom beak making chatter, claws tap dancing on the chairs back, barely containing his anticipation.

"Are the two of you ready for that, for the unbridled attention?" Jani laughed.

"Yes," they replied, eyes wide, waiting for her to give them more instruction.

"Can the two of you make recollections of what once was, what could be, and what should have been without getting *too* caught up in it?"

"Yes," they shouted in unison.

"Then let's go for it!" Jani said, shaking her fist in the air as Francisco followed suit and Max let out a screech in affirmation.

"But are we going to be able to do this," Francisco asked, "when you know *only* bad Spanish and I know *only* a little English?"

Max expressed his displeasure with Francisco for making a doubting comment, purple feathers held flat on the crest of his head.

"La Jefita (pet name for boss) would be *dead* by the time you learned English, Francisco." Max crudely snapped. "*I* can't help write the book, even though I would love too, as *I* only have wingtips to write with, but I will still help Jani as best I can, even if you can't!"

"Hold it, my young ones," Jani told them. "Francisco will be speaking English by the time I write this book and my hair will be white by then, as white as snow!"

"But that will take you *forever*, Jani. I will be an old bird by then. Your hair is now bright red!"

"You will still be young when the time comes, Maximo. Parrots can live to be eighty. We will write that book before you know it... you see, a startling red is what happens when you put red dye on pure white hair. There is no other way you can get a color as stunning as mine, but it is time for a change, as I don't want anyone looking at white roots while I am lying in my casket."

"YES! ...I mean, NO," Max replied, confusion causing his feathers to quiver as a chill came over him.

12

Decision to Write

Max had experienced death as ones number coming up, or in the case of death of one of a pair, as birds balancing on a teeter- totter, one inexplicably falling off into an abys, leaving the bird on the other side alone and stunned, the death unplanned, unaccountable. He felt unsettled by this shift, from the three of them becoming famous, to this talk about death. He didn't want to outlive Jani and Francisco, and he didn't want them to outlive him. Why did Jani keep bringing up tomorrow, what did tomorrow have to do with today... on the other hand why write a book if there was no tomorrow? Max took another step into the ocean of humanity, as the thought of losing Jani or Francisco made a stab into his heart, into the special place once reserved only for Teo. His love for Francisco, however, took on larger dimensions, ones with a faculty for communication that went beyond the perimeters of possibility, but to those who witnessed it, very real.

Jani's small book expanded into one of grander proportions as her dream list of expectations grew. She fantasized about writing a book whose pages unfolded as lessons on living, a flower whose shed petals drifted like words of wisdom that could be re-gathered on a still night. They could be retrieved, and be there for her when her memory failed, when she could no longer type accurate words on paper. She could use them to fill out her manuscript, the story of how they built their nest from strands of each of their individual identities. Max came from a different species. He was genetically a bird. Francisco came from an ancient Mexican culture. They had seemed so different from Jani, who had retired to Mexico's subtropical highlands thirteen years earlier yet they came together to create a valuable life by being united in their need to find safety and acceptance. "Yes," Jani thought, "It was a story waiting to be told."

Jani, Francisco, and Max lived together outside the confines of traditional thinking. Others who observed them thought their relationship looked surreal; some wondered what it was *they* were missing. Perhaps the peace that was lived at Aztec Studios was built on the foundation of an environmental art form, one whose medium of hope transcended negative reasoning; perhaps it fell together like pickup sticks.

"But what do you want us to do right now?" Max fussed, "...while we are waiting for you to write this book?"

"Why we just go on living, *silly bird*, playing out life like we always do!" Jani responded.

Max glanced over at their two cats dumbly staring out the window, as one of them, Isabella, looked over at him in her usual snit. He was glad she hadn't mentioned *them* to be included in the book, those ordinary cats with no dimension.

The stars sprinkled the heavens on that night, blessing their habitat. It was a place where they created art, where Francisco wove original tapestries by hand, where Jani painted scenes of Mexican life and portraits of those she loved, and made surreal collages of the mystique of ancient Mexico's beliefs; narratives brought into the modern world. It was a home where Francisco studied and began to bloom, a place to dye wool in the street with Max helping them, the place where they laughed and sang and where one day Max would learn to warble.

"We are going to be off on an exciting journey of recollections," Jani told Max Bird and Francisco."

"Feel the moon's glow, the warmth between us, and the magic of life. We must always remember this night, because it is a night of perfection, it is proof that perfection does exist." Max rolled his eyes, his lids gently closing over them in bliss.

Darkness was falling as they lounged on their rooftop lookout, whiffs of jasmine drifting up from a neighbor's courtyard below, moisture from the air barely dusting the hairs on Jani and Francisco's skin, Max's feathers turning iridescent in the coming light of the moon.

Back of kitchen overlooking great room. "If I had hands,
I'd help you with the dishes." Max told Francisco

3
Clipped Wings

"I have forgotten how to fly, Jefita," Max said, looking for the truth yet hoping she would not expose it.

"Am I still a bird if I can't fly? If I am not a bird, then what am I?"

Max, perched on Francisco's shoulder, sat waiting for Jani's reply. But she didn't need to make one, as Max had known the truth since the day before…that as sure as the full moon would appear each month, Francisco would hold him as if in embrace, covering his head against his chest so Max could not see, and would stretch out one of his wings, then the other, as Jani silently snipped off his wing feathers. Returning the scissors to where they had been hidden, the interlude would end and they would continue on with their day as if nothing had happened.

When Max, eyes bared, had at last solemnly witnessed his own clipping, he would not at first accept the reality of it, as he still preferred to blame his inability to fly on himself rather than to accept the fact that those he loved had altered him. He had witnessed the sorrow in Francisco's soft eyes and the look of anguish on Jani's face when she watched her own fingers let go of the cut ends of his feathers and watched them flutter into the waste basket.

Clipped Wings

"Hiding the truth does not work because in the end it requires lies that keep feeding on themselves," Jani said at the time, as a simple statement of fact, concealing her desire to hold Max and tell him how sorry she was, wanting the three of them to be able to cry together, but knowing that they needed her to be their anchor.

Jani had wanted to continue to deny the clipping of Max in her old familiar way, but the existence of its reality tugged at them like an undertow. Truth held up in front of a mirror can scorch the eyes. A family's secrets are often kept out of love, because to reveal them would be a risk to all the trust they had formed and all that would follow, but secrets held so close endlessly plague the memory and ensnarl it in a tangle of traps.

"You did the right thing, Jani," Francisco said, seeing her slumped down in a chair before the empty television screen. Max is an adult now; it is time for him to know the truth.

Max was in his element living in the middle of an artist's studio, that is, if there ever was an "element" for a bird caught on the edge of a reality foreign to the wild world he had come from. It was Maestro Francisco's, too, who having lost the years of his life between 14 and 42, was, aggravatingly for Jani, just now learning how to screw in a light bulb.

Jani herself understood cages, their elusiveness, their lack of corners to get trapped in, the seductiveness of their totality, and their lack of a back door. This awareness was the great common denominator among the three of them. They rarely wanted to leave their cage, their unique environment insulating them against the thrust of the life outside that did not suit them. They preferred to view the world beyond it as if seen through a veil.

18

Clipped Wings

Cages come in all different forms, sizes and descriptions. The one Max Bird lived in, together with Jani and Francisco, was therefore not the exception to any rule, but was on the fringe of what a cage description could entail. Jani designed their art gallery and weaving studios just for them, a unique place where they lived, and although when she ran into another artist she sometimes referred to it as "Environmental Art," the three of them knew it was really their cage, containing a nest for each that gave them the utmost satisfaction. Francisco sometimes thought Jani had designed their live-work space to keep her confined, as if she, too, were a bird, to keep those confined with her to herself, so that she would have company on the creative ventures that occupied her mind. Francisco was satisfied with this arrangement but on occasion restlessness would overtake Max.

"I dream, oh how I dream," Max muttered as the sun began to set.

Francisco held Max securely on his rare visit to swing with him on the rooftop hammock, a venture for Max that always left Jani very nervous. She knew that Max loved them but also that he had romantic dreams about flying off into the heavens, the lead bird in a flock of those migrating, like the pelicans that migrated across the lake every year. She noticed Max as he watched the birds in the distance, the ridges where his wings attached to his shoulders rising and falling in tune to the beat of their wings as they ascended, soaring up into the heavens, migrating north in the spring, living out their destiny. Jani would have let him go if he could do that, but he was not a pelican, he was a parrot, one from a different climate than where he now lived, a species accustomed to heat and humidity, living amid the canopy of trees yet needing the midday sun, birds that grouped

19

socializing with their families, never venturing far from their place of birth.

Jani felt Max needed to understand his history as a parrot to know that if his wings grew back, with his impulsive nature, he would fly off and Francisco would not be there to put him inside at night and cover him up so he would be warm, and in a short time he would die and they would suffer the loss of the most unique of all parrots and it would leave a hole in their hearts.

"I wish I could be a pelican," Max confided to Francisco, "like those that migrate across the lake in the far horizon coming in all grouped together yet free, the wind picking up the skirts of their tail feathers as they are about to land on the water, tickling the edges of their concealed down. When I think about it I get so excited that if you were not holding me tight I would attempt to fly off this mirador [rooftop lookout] this very moment, even knowing I would go straight down into the neighbor's nesting chickens, even knowing how much I would miss you, and miss the joy of how you hold me as we swing on this hammock above the whole world."

"What do you dream about, Maestro?" Max inquired as Francisco, with his forefinger, flipped up the feathers on the back of Max's neck.

"Why, I dream about becoming a parrot like you!" Francisco replied, caught off guard, and only half in jest. "To be enveloped in another's arms at night, have *my* neck scratched, to watch someone else wash the dishes, to receive attention every time *I* squawked, to be given the title of Public Relations Director and get the *tons* of the publicity that you do!"

"And live in a cage like me?" Max twirled his head around to peck at Francisco's collar to make his point. "You have got to be kidding!"

"No I'm not. Are you squawking about your cage in the garden, the one downstairs with no door? Real cages have doors, Max, or are you squawking about your antique cage inside, where Jani covers you with a special satin throw at night, the one that I remove after your first peep in the morning. You know, that cage that you are so anxious to go into when you get sleepy. I would be very content if *I* was covered up in a special blanket and tucked in at night!"

"If I had arms I would help you with the dishes, Maestro, and I would tuck you in and I would hug you, I would hug you a lot!" Max exclaimed as he leaned into Francisco, stretching out a wing in an attempt to comfort him.

"We are lucky, Maxie. Sometimes I feel so alone even though I know I'm not, because I have you to hold in my lonely times."

Max's feathers puffed up in a display of happiness on hearing Francisco's words as he confided to him, "I like it so much when we sneak up here past Jani, up high in the sky where she does not want me to be."

New rooftop lookout. "We will be able to see the whole world spread out before us, as far as the eye can see!" Jani exclaimed

4

Peanuts & Ice Cream

Jani stepped out onto the small porch that extended from the back of their second floor and looked down into the neighbor's lot below. It was where the old ranchero who farmed it kept his horse, now ridden only in parades, and his 58 chickens, but Jani did not really see them as her thoughts were elsewhere. Her focus was on developing a plan to put an addition on the only spot on their property she had not yet built on, the flat roof that housed the skylights that lit up the great room below.

Standing there, tape in hand at the foot of the stairway leading to the roof, Jani mused, 'We would have a three hundred and sixty degree view of the Sierra Madre to the west, the picturesque village of Ajijic to the east, with Lake Chapala sprawled out like a panorama before us. We could watch the fishermen cast their nets out into the lake as the sun peeked out from hiding, and watch the sun go back in at night. Before us would be the whole world as far as the eye could see! It could all be ours in one fell swoop. All I need to do is to build six steps up from the floor of the Mirador and it is a done deal!' Jani headed up to the rooftop to measure.

Max's eyes pinpointed in and out in alarm as he and Francisco heard the clomp-clomp of Jani's feet on the metal staircase. Their great time swinging in the hammock on the rooftop mirador was about to come to an abrupt end, as Jani's feet were rising on the steps too quickly for them to halt the momentum that they built up on the hammock as they dangerously swung out over the railing so they could count the number of chickens clucking below.

"What are you guys doing up here," Jani hollered, but her heart helplessly softened at the sight of them so peacefully swinging in the hammock suspended in the air, backlit by the azure blue of the clearest sky.

Francisco smiled in sweet anticipation of a scolding. He coveted attention from Jani in any form and really appreciated being singled out for the talking *to* that he and Max were about to receive.

"I feel uneasy about you bringing Max up here," Jani scolded Francisco. He yearns to be like those migrating birds he sees landing on the water across the lake."

"But I like to yearn," Max interrupted.

"In a split second he could go over that railing in an impulsive attempt to join them and would wind up falling three stories right onto the metal roof of the neighbors' chicken coop and break his neck!"

"But if you didn't clip my wings, I would just land on it nicely, Jefita," Max said.

"I am sorry Max," Jani replied, her lips tightening in resolution, "but your wings have to be clipped."

"Max is an adult bird now, Jani you still treat him as if he were a child. You do the same thing to me. Times change and nowadays it is often me that is protecting you *and* Max.!"

"On top of everything else I am responsible for around here," Jani went on, having paid no attention to what Francisco just said, "you expect me to witness you wandering around on our verandas open to the sky with an impulsive bird perched on your shoulder, one who will inevitably fly off. That is way too much to expect of me. I need you *both* to be more mature. I need you, Francisco, to stop lolling around when I am not looking!"

"Max is not just *any* bird," Francisco continued. "You don't give him enough credit. You're not being fair."

"Life is not fair," was Jani's quick retort. "It is not fair to you, to me, or to Max. We all pay a price in this life, and he pays his in feathers, that's all. And I am tired of being the hard guy in this household!"

But Jani realized what Francisco was saying was true, that Max was an exception in the cast of living creatures, that first and foremost he was Max, an extension of them, a warm blooded creature that they had brought into their world, one that had adjusted in an extraordinary way, a true exception to any rule of nature. She and Francisco lived together in the gallery because that was their choice, because they knew about life on the outside, and they knew how life in their insulated area suited them just right as it shielded them against harshness of values they could no longer adjust to. Max belonged with them, of that she was sure, but she knew that Max had to learn these things by himself for him to live among them with the same rich satisfaction they felt. She knew this to be true but no matter how many times she thought it over, she could not figure out how. For Max to be on the outside would be his death sentence.

"Max mustn't feel like we own him," Francisco told Jani, sad that she was the one who had to bear the brunt of the responsibility for him, Max, and the gallery, wishing he could take on some of it himself, could become the equal partner he felt she dreamed of.

"Francisco, please take Max downstairs," Jani said, retreating down the metal staircase. She hollered back up when she reached the bottom, "See what's on *National Geographic*, Max likes that!"

"I don't like National Geographic, I like...." Max hollered down to her before Francisco had a chance to cover his beak.

"Look, don't make more problems. I know how to handle this. *I* am an expert at diverting Jani's attention, just watch me!" Francisco whispered to Max, trying to make it sound like he was not bragging.

Max thought they were heading for the television set, but as they paused in the garden, Francisco pulled on the clangor of the heavy brass bell that hung down into the courtyard.

"What is it?" Jani hollered down from two floors above.

"We're going to the store, Max is out of peanuts," Francisco answered.

Jani scurried down the stairs to catch them. Max and Francisco were half way up the street before she was able to holler out the front door. They had stopped and turned around before she even reached it, waiting for her to appear as she always did.

"Bring me back a Dove ice cream bar, chocolate coating; Vanilllaaa!!" Jani screamed, cupping her hands around her mouth so they would be sure to hear.

Jani smiled as she watched them continue down the road, her two precious companions who were so vulnerable in the outside world. She tried not to think of all the bad things that could happen to them.

"We are lucky, Max. We are unique, there is none else like us." Francisco laughed.

"Especially me!" Max exclaimed.

"We are artists! Jani says that artists need to support each other. She said that being an artist usually means spending a life creating alone, but she is not alone anymore, Max, because she has us to help her."

"I have a great idea, Maestro. I thought of it the other day, actually, I got all aflutter at the idea of it. Jani had on that blouse, the one with the orange and red roses, and different kinds of berries printed all over it; she had just taken it from the dryer and it still smelled of softener when she put it on."

"Yes, I remember, it smelled good," Francisco replied.

"Well, anyway," Max continued, "I was thinking that the three of us could start sleeping together at night in Jani's big bed. Boy! That would be *real* cozy and make us feel good. I will ask her, Maestro, I'll bet she will think that is a great idea!"

"Look, Max, I wouldn't ask her if I were you."

"But why not?"

"There are things you just don't understand about humans, about relationships and stuff."

"Like what kind of stuff?"

"Don't you get tired of asking questions, Max? Sometimes you make me feel *very* uncomfortable."

"Let's play run and flap, okay, Maestro? That's always fun!"

Francisco held onto each of Max's short legs as if they were handles as Max folded his talons as best he could under the circumstances, and then they were off and running down the street, Francisco holding Max aloft like a rising kite as he flapped his wings wildly, neck stretched out, beak pointed into the wind. They ran and ran until they were both out of breath and came to a stop in front of the store and rested on the step in front of it, Max laughing a loud human laugh.

"I love to feel free! I love the exhilaration of it. I love the wind blowing in my face. Someday maybe I can fly to the store beside you, we can have a race. Is that possible, Maestro?"

"I don't know. Instincts are very hard to control, Max. Even humans under the best of circumstances fall victim to following their instincts, even when it destroys themselves and their families. If you got distracted and flew away from me, you might forget that you cannot land on water and would sink to the bottom and drown, or maybe a preying animal in the bush might eat you, or maybe a big snake would bite you or a scorpion—there are a lot of those around here hiding under the rocks. It is not as great as you think to be free."

"Maybe you know that, but I don't, and I want to fly with all of my feathers!"

"I hope you can someday, but first you must show more maturity, Max. You must prove yourself to be a competent bird, one who is able to make good decisions. Then maybe you can convince Jani that you don't need to have your wings clipped anymore, but you must be patient, very patient because that takes time."

"I think Jani would like a strawberry ice cream bar better, don't you, Maestro? Let's buy her a strawberry one, that one there," he pointed with one wing feather. "It's covered in crunchies!" Max exclaimed with such enthusiasm that Francisco quickly pulled the freezer door closed after he retrieved Jani's Dove bar.

"I love strawberries," Max exclaimed, as they headed out the door.

Max and Francisco "hanging out".
"Maturity is not a destination,
it's a layering process." Francisco explained.

5
Maturity Takes Time

"I need to get to maturity fast, Maestro. How do I get on the right road?" Max asked Francisco.

"Maturity is not a destination, Max, it's a layering process. It can't be rushed. If you are ever going to do more than just flap your clipped wings, however, you are going to have to make more progress than you have been."

"Do you mean layered like the layers of a cake? I don't understand. What it is it I am supposed to be layering?" Max said, as they stood before the cash register at the neighborhood tienda, waiting for the peanuts and the ice cream to be bagged.

They sat down in front of the store beside a barrel of mops and brooms side lit by strokes of red and green florescent color from the soft drink signs hanging in the store window. Francisco set the bag down and Max sat on his knee facing him, looking directly into his eyes both were cracking open fresh peanuts and munching on them as they began to talk.

"Are being wise and being mature the same?" Max pondered, posing a question that Francisco again had to stretch his mind to answer.

Maturity Takes Time

"It's not possible to have wisdom if you don't have maturity, Max. Pretend your book is transparent and you can look through the thickness of all of its pages and see patterns where thoughts take form and then apply them in the most astute way—Good grief, Max, is that me talking? What does astute mean? These words are just tumbling out of nowhere. Do you understand what I am saying?"

"I *do* understand you, Maestro, I *always* understand you," Max said, at that moment believing it.

Jani brought out a plastic chair and set it on the sidewalk as she waited for her companions to return. When they came up the street, Max and Francisco were enthusiastically carrying on a conversation. Jani took pleasure in hearing the fullness of Francisco's vocabulary, which never failed to surprise her coming from this man who once was too insecure to utter a single sentence. Her heart soared in pride. Francisco loved it when Jani waited for him out in the street like that. He sweetly handed her the Dove bar, which she carried upstairs to eat in her favorite chair in the great room.

Jani recalled how far Francisco had come in such a short time. It was like a miracle… and what a good teacher he was to Max, almost fatherly… and how Francisco had such a serious face, not at all like his father, Teo.

Jani and Teo's different version of maturity was the main reason they separated. A mature man, Teo felt, could work endless days in the fields and never drop, entrust his life to coyotes, and not know if he would live to see his family again, and never complain about it. A mature man never cried, always drank his tequila straight and never lost his smile. Teo's smile had been his shield. Jani knew he was filled with deep wounds but the identity of them she never learned, for his armor had been air tight.

Maturity Takes Time

Jani had begun to hate Teo's smile that had once drawn her in so tight. In the end, his weavings all had serious mistakes. She felt he was making them deliberately. One day while he was weaving she confronted him. He wore a blank smile. Raising her arm and pulling it back, ready to impulsively hit him, she was stunned by her own capacity to be violent. She dropped her arm. She still remembers the look of shock on Teo's face.

Francisco knew from the beginning that Jani was kind, even when she at first refused to let him live in her home, let him take root in her heart, but even at that time she washed Francisco's clothes, took him to the doctor when he was sick, made sure he had food, and allowed him to use her shower. But Max was just beginning to understand. He was confused by her periods of anger.

Almost a year had gone by since she jumped up and down on the DVD player. She and Teo were returning home from the tianguis [street market]. He leaned back in the passenger seat as she drove home, a blissful smile on his face. Teo was holding the bag of DVD's in his lap. She misinterpreted his mood and suggested a walk along the beach to savor the breeze, watch the cranes in repose as the water washed to shore, a custom they once had. Her suggestion was met with no response. Jani pulled up in front of their studios. Teo jumped out, and clutching onto the bag, raced inside and pulled his chair up the television set as if it were a dinner table and *he* was the only one eating. Then he put in the disk. His nose almost pressed against the screen. He was full of anticipation. Jani stepped in front of him and turned off the television. He continued to sit there as if it was still running. Jani smashed the DVD player, jumping up and down on it for effect. The next day Teo's smile was less true than usual.

33

Maturity Takes Time

Max at first blamed Jani for her and Teo's conflicts.... All Teo wanted to do was to watch his favorite television programs. He was willing to do anything she told him. He always spoke sweet words. Max wondered, *why did she tell him he had to go?* Then he looked at Francisco and posed another question.

"Why did she let *you* stay, Maestro?" he asked.

"She told me it was because I remembered to take out the trash without being told," Francisco replied with a wry smile. But even then, Max suspected the truth.

Jani had taken Francisco into her heart years ago. She and Teo had been living in one room while she was having the gallery built. Her heart ached for Francisco when he slept on their roof during the rainy season under an inverted plastic swimming pool, when he drew his doves of peace on her walls, when his morning face looked ravaged from voices crying in the distance, when he thought a man was attacking his cousin, when he mistakenly protected her and they had to commit him, when he lived in a mine shaft in the mountain and she and Teo had brought him food, when he made her the stairway up to it so she wouldn't fall, when others destroyed it, when she discovered that he could talk, and then discovered that he could weave, but most of all after she bought him a loom and set it up in the front yard under a tarp where he stood sheltered from the broiling sun weaving and singing, *"Happy Birthday to me, Happy birthday to me...."*

It had not been possible for Jani to let go of Francisco. She folded up the wrapper of her ice cream bar and walked into the kitchen to get a coke. Returning, she sat back down in her chair, put her feet up on the foot stool, and heaved a satisfied sigh. The hum of Max and Francisco's voices talking downstairs gave her satisfaction, as did the ambience of the great room. It served as an additional gallery if someone that was particularly interested in their work came in, and of course, if it was reasonably clean on that day. Those coming into the room for the first time were mesmerized by the stunning views of the mountains from the front veranda to the north and the panorama of Ajijic and volcanic lake from the porch to the south. The views were so distracting that sometimes those that visited did not notice the display of fine weavings and paintings.

A couple came in. Francisco and Max showed them their gallery and Francisco's weaving studio downstairs. They invited the couple up to the great room. Jani took her feet off the footstool and smoothed her hair. Max and Francisco preceded the couple as they entered. Max flit over and perched hopefully on the end of a rack of their favorite Maya influenced tapestries stretching out a wing, motioning to the couple to take a look. Francisco unclipped a hanger, proudly stretching a fine tapestry out to its fullest length.

"This one is beautiful, violet, with creams and rich earth tones," Max chirped enticingly as the woman looked at it smiling in nodded appreciation. But her husband had spotted the panoramic view of the ancient fishing village, the church's steeple calling out to him to take a closer look as it rose above the town and the shimmering lake. He took his wife's arm and led her to the glass wall where they admired the view, forgetting all about Max, Francisco *and* the tapestries.

"Ohh, what a wonderful view," they exclaimed in unison. "You don't mind if we step outside to have a better look, do you?"

Jani remembered the lacy pink brassieres she had draped over a hanger just out of sight. She had placed a kerchief in

35

front of them in modesty because of Max and Francisco, but now she recalled how her cat Elliot had knocked the kerchief off and how she had meant to replace it.

"I am sorry. The back porch is closed today," she replied to the disappointed couple, with an unintentional sigh, trying to hide her exasperation.

Insulted by Jani's rebuff and with a huff, they marched past Francisco, almost brushing Max off his shoulder in their hurry to make an exit. Max called out after them, chirping a hollow, "Please come back." He had tried his best to show Jani, the Maestro, and himself that he was in control of his growing maturity.

"It's my fault they left," Max lamented. "I failed. If I hadn't brought them up here they may have bought the tapestry downstairs that they liked. Maybe if I hadn't showed them the violet one, if I had shown them the earth colored one first, no, I mean, I should not have shown them the violet one since he didn't like blue... it would have been better if.... I am trying, Jefita, I am really trying!" Max squawked.

"Just because you didn't meet with success doesn't mean you did anything wrong, Max. I think you did fine job, *really fine*. Maybe *my* voice had an edge to it and that chased them off, I don't know."

Francisco said you would let me grow my feathers out if I became mature enough, Jefita, is that true? Max inquired, eager to change the subject, the pupils of his eyes flickering in anticipation.

"Everything in this life is possible, Max, but it's even more possible if you have a realistic plan and work at it."

"I am a bird with clipped wings, Jefita. A bird that cannot fly is not a bird. I think the idea of a plan I can work on is a *real* good idea. Where do I get one? I would rather have a

36

plan to prove to you that I would not fly away if I could, than to develop maturity. Maturity would take me way too much time!"

Elliot looking up at Max. They had no idea Max had
been concealing all of that anger under his feathers

38

6
Implosion of Words

"I remember the first day we heard Max talk, Jani, do you remember?"

"Yes. How long was it now, two, three years? That was a crazy day, Francisco, unbelievable... and distressing."

"Remember how mad Max got at Teo? We had no idea he had been concealing all of that anger under his feathers!" Jani said.

Francisco and Jani were used to seeing Max mope around on the days Teo was to come. He would wait for him to come bobbing in the front gate, singing out as he approached with his usual melodious lilt. For a long time Max's longing to see Teo, to hear the sound of his voice, and inhale the smell of his sweet straw sombrero persisted, only to be let down when Teo arrived, hardly noticing Max's presence.

"I dread seeing Max all drooped over like that. It breaks my heart." Jani had told Francisco. Maybe birds never stop mourning."

"But he looks very strange this morning, not at all like he usually does when Teo is coming." Francisco replied. "Look at how long he has his neck stretched out as he stares at the wall in back of his cage."

Max was thinking about his sister Tweet. Their vendor in Jocotepec had bought them at auction in the thieves market in Guadalajara, such a lowly place for a bird in as fine a feather as Tweet. She was a perfect bird, did not have a mangled foot like he did. When she was sold he felt like he was the only parrot left in the whole world and unsuccessfully tried to bond with the canaries, whose cages the vendor had all roped together as he marched them up and down the village streets hollering, "pajaros, bonitos chicos pajaros."

The vendor had put Tweet into a brown paper sack, and folding the top over, handed it to a little girl in white socks who was clutching onto her father's hand. Max screamed, "Come back, come back, Tweet. Don't leave me here to be a parrot all alone!" The little girl looked back at him as if she understood, but her father gave her a little tug and they walked away.

Max had that same sense of abandonment when Teo left, but as time went on he became more and more angry. There was a very big difference in the way they left. Teo could have looked back and said goodbye. Tweet couldn't. The more he thought about this, the more he stared at the wall.

"When Teo comes today I will tell him he has to pay more attention to Max. I cannot imagine how he can come in here and walk by Max like he doesn't exist!" Jani said.

"Do you love Max?" Francisco asked.

"Yes I do," Jani replied.

"I love him too," Francisco said.

Max had been listening. His heart swelled upon hearing their words. He looked up and saw their cat Elliot posing against the skywalk, the tips of his fur shimmering in the midday sun. He imagined Isabella, Elliot's female counterpart, flopping against a nearby wall eyeing a fly. Jani and Francisco were smiling at him. Max realized Jani and Francisco were birds too, birds with flapping hands instead of wings, birds that also could not fly, that called out to him in a universal language; birds of a family true to him, birds of love. Max also understood that a great part of him had become human; he was part of the human condition, even though he accepted the fact that he entered their world under a severe handicap. He looked again at Elliot and knew that Isabella was nearby and that they were also part of his family. That special moment of revelation, however, was interrupted when Teo walked in the front door.

"Hola," Teo cheerily called up to Jani and Francisco in the kitchen above. He stopped in the courtyard next to Max's cage, not intrusive, yet hoping Jani would invite him in.

"Hi, Teo, ¿cómo estás?" Jani had hollered down from the skywalk. She tried to be pleasant, as he was a basically good person, but her angst overtook her when she spotted Teo's polyester pants with pressed creases, the dark sunglasses he was wearing to protect his eyes, and the slouch of his shoulders since he had retired from weaving,

He was a project that had gone awry. Jani felt he had cost her not only a lot of money but six irretrievable years of her life. She bared her teeth and whispered to Francisco, "I just can't deal with him today and be decent! You're going to have to, he's your father! Go down, tell him I am sorry, that I am busy, and to *please* visit with Max before he leaves!"

"¿Cómo estás, hijo?" Teo said, hugging his son in a tender way, but one that kept a little distance.

"This is for you," Teo said, handing Francisco a bag of hot roasted chicken, just off the spit. The smell of it, delectable and taste inspiring, drifted up to Jani. She loved roasted chicken and was thankful he brought it as she was no longer in the mood to cook.

"Thank you, Teo," she hollered down.

"De nada, mi amor," he called back, refusing to let go of his pet name for her.

It had seemed like an ordinary day, Teo handing Francisco a bag of roasted chicken as they exchanged greetings. Teo had become accustomed to ignoring the presence of Max, who was gagging from the smell of burnt bird flesh as he perched in his cage at their side. His small body had an emotional upheaval brewing as the conflicting emotions of love, grief, joy and anger that he had just experienced were on a collision course and were about to explode in the form of words.

It was strange that Francisco and Teo were simultaneously aware a change of dynamics was about to take place in their midst. They both turned to look at Max, and at the same time, Jani looked down from the kitchen above. They were to witness Max's metamorphosis from the ventriloquist like speech expected of a parrot to that of a human. As they watched, Max opened his beak a few times, and then screwing his face up in a forced and critical effort to speak looked up at Jani. As if he sought affirmation, his eyes reached hers, and gazed upon them with a sacred expression, yet one of inquiry, and in a most a resonant and human voice, Max burst into a fury and hollered up a question that shocked them all.

"So, how would Teo like it if I gave him roasted human for *his* comida?" Max screamed in perfect English, shaking with an intensity that spewed feathered down that settled on Teo's sombrero. "Maybe human breasts, barbacoa style, ah, ha, ha, ha," he laughed, swirling his head around to confront

Teo, his bird eyes spinning aggressively as he choked back more hysteria. Teo, who had no taste for complications, backed out the front entrance and left.

Francisco had understood that voices could come out of nowhere, but Jani was startled. She looked down at Francisco for an explanation. He hung onto the bag of chicken as he climbed the stairs, entered the kitchen, and faced Jani. "Have you heard him talk before?" Jani whispered. The look on Francisco's face gave her the answer.

"I might as well live alone. How could you have kept this from me?"

"You didn't ask," Francisco tried to explain. "I thought you didn't want to know, and besides, I thought you might already know. If you wore your hearing aids you wouldn't feel so left out, Jani. As time went on it became harder and harder to tell you, that's all!"

"How can he sound so human? How can it be explained?"

The miracle of Max Bird never could be explained, but a Mexican ornithologist once told Jani he could see the face of Jesus printed into the pupils of Max's eyes. He believed this even after Jani explained that Max was anything but a saint.

It was through Isabella Cat and Elliot that Max first identified the feeling of guilt. "Creatures," he said, "that were incapable of feeling it themselves."

7
Guilt and Chicken

"We shouldn't have left Jani out in the cold like we did, Francisco. We should have prepared her for the fact that I was talking, yet, what could we do?"

"We could have been honest and just told her, Max."

"But I didn't understand it! How could I explain it to Jani?" Max twerped, scratching at his ear. "How could I make her understand what neither of us had ever experienced before?"

"Your voice is so...human," Francisco replied. "and appealing, in an adolescent way. Let's face it, Max, maybe Jani didn't need an explanation; maybe she just needed to be told."

Max felt regret about keeping a secret from Jani, but foremost in his mind was the fact that Francisco had carried the bag of chicken upstairs to the kitchen... and his fear that Jani would eat it...which...being a bird himself... he felt he could never accept.

"I feel like I could burst into a thousand feathers! Jani simply cannot eat that chicken! It can't be! I cannot live with a fowl-eating cannibal. You wouldn't eat it, now that you realize that it would be the same as eating a member of my bird family, would you, Maestro?"

Guilt and Chicken

"But, Max, you must understand that Jani and I are carnivores. For us eating meat that comes from other creatures is normal."

"I'm glad that Jani knows I *can* talk in human language," Max said. "Now I can explain to her why she can't eat chicken. The problem is, Jani does not think of herself as being the final one in a fowl's food chain. She thoughtlessly condones the murder of innocent chickens! If she had thought about it, she would *never* do that."

Francisco dangled the bag containing the roasted chicken in front of Jani's nose when he entered the kitchen. "What are we going to do with this?" he whispered so that Max, perched on his cage below them, could not hear.

"Why…we are going to eat it, Francisco!"

"But we can't do that!"

"I am starving, Francisco, just give me a leg, he will never know!"

"Max will smell it on your breath."

"Give me a leg! Give it to me NOW!" Jani snapped, grabbing the bag away from him, salivating.

Celiac disease is an illness Jani had carried with her for a lifetime. When she was a little girl she had not been able to jump rope; her legs had not picked up. She had sat in the crook of an apple tree during recess fighting exhaustion. Her body did not absorb vitamins so her stomach growled in hunger.

Jani was sixty four before they found out what was wrong with her. Her intestines had become smooth inside, like plumbing; food she ate left her stomach as quickly as it was put in. There was only skin left on her bones. She was not appealing.

Guilt and Chicken

That was when Teo had still lived with Jani. The humiliation she had felt surpassed her physical pain because Teo used buckets like they were diaper pails (as only a father of thirteen could)to wash her soiled underwear and linens out by hand as if she were a baby. During bad dreams she cried out in defense of her babies, even though at that time they were middle aged men. Teo always listened to her.
How could she not eat his gift of chicken?

"What are we going to do about Max?" Francisco said sitting across the kitchen table from Jani as she grabbed a wing. "Shouldn't we talk to him?"

"How much out of the ordinary can I be expected to adjust to?" Jani replied between chews. "Why do I have to facilitate comfortableness for others in unordinary circumstances? *You* go keep Max company and let me eat in peace!"

"I don't hear voices anymore, Jani. You don't have to worry about *me* anymore. I no longer cry in the night. Life here has been normal for some time."

"Tell me, did Max speak to us in English or in Spanish?"

"Spanish," Francisco replied.

"That's what I was afraid of. I heard him in English. The mystery becomes more complex." As Jani reached for a drumstick, Francisco soothed her head, as Mexican men do when they love their mothers too much.

"Since you refuse to eat, Francisco, cut the left-over chicken into bite size pieces, lay it on the bottom of the casserole...and top it with frozen peas. Make some instant mashed potatoes to cover it. We will stick it inside the freezer. On another day we can pop it in the micro. That will be the end of *that* chicken, at least for today, okay?"

Guilt and Chicken

Max was perched with his head buried into the feathers of his breast when Francisco went back down to see how he was doing. He pulled his beak out for a moment and asked Francisco a simple question, "Is Jani eating the chicken?"

"Jani has always eaten chicken. Why are you so upset now?"

"I never thought of roasted chicken as being another bird, since it came in a bag, Maestro. I didn't think of it being killed, of having its head chopped and its guts pulled out. I didn't think about its feathers being thrown to the wind, or made into a pillow."

"Look at it this way. Would we ask you to stop pulling worms out of the soil and gobbling them up raw... and how about bugs? How many of those have you eaten? How do you know they don't have feelings...and the grass and all kinds of growing things, aren't they also made of energy...maybe they have feelings too. See how flowers open up with the sun and wither when it gets cold?"

Max tucked his beak back into his breast feathers. The neighbor's rooster crowed. Max was humped over like an old man as he turned his back to Francisco.

The chicken did not have time to become frozen when Jani's stomach began to growl, hungry as usual. Francisco could not get the uneaten casserole out of his mind, he put Max to bed early.

Jani's cat, Elliot, stood between her and Francisco at one end of the round table as the three of them feasted. Francisco's cat, Isabella, sat at a respectful distance frowning, putting only a slight pall on their sinful repast.

"Meow," Elliot cried with his chin balanced on the top of the table, slapping the tabletop with his paw as if it were a yardstick. He demanded another piece of chicken, preferably white meat. Jani fished a piece from her plate with the tip of

48

her finger and offered it to him. He sniffed at it delicately, expecting it to measure up to the finest wine for his ingestion, then turned up his nose.

"That piece has mashed potatoes on it. You know he doesn't like potatoes," Francisco told Jani.

Isabella dutifully ate the cat food that was set out before her, never dreaming of bothering Jani, Francisco, or Elliot as they were eating. Isabella stood her ground on preserving the sanctity of her own eating habits. She only allowed Elliot to eat from the same bowl as herself if he reached his paw into the dish and dragged a morsel out to eat on the floor, one piece at a time.

The following day Isabella lounged on Jani's lap as they watched the news. She laid vertically, paws wrapped around Jani's neck in the habit of a small child, with her wet nose against Jani's ear as she drooled on the nape of her neck. Jani tried to hide her disgust but was unable to dislodge the creature because Isabella loved her so much. Isabella controlled Jani by guilt. Jani's dislike of Isabella multiplied because of that fact. It was only Francisco that loved Isabella, but she felt suffocated by Francisco's affection.

Jani was turned off by Isabella because she was sulky, because she didn't pick up her scrawny tail, or even perk her ears, and her tiger stripes never became fully developed, giving her a dish rag look. Max studied them, sniffing the resentment Jani had for Isabella. That was when he first identified the feeling of guilt and the power it could wield when held in the hands of a conniving cat, especially one like Isabella who was actually incapable of feeling it herself. He wondered what one did with the feeling of guilt. Did they spend it? Leave it there to rot? They must do something with it. And then he began to feel it within himself.

8
Letter to Tweet

Max watched Jani write letters to her sister. He noticed that she never put them in an envelope, that they were never mailed. He saw her tuck them away in a locked drawer.

"Why are you writing letters that you don't send?" Max asked.

"I don't write them to send, Max. I write them to get things that are bothering me off my chest."

Max decided it was time to feel more human, to extract the truths that he, Max Bird, had been denied. "I have things that need to be said too, things that have been bothering me. I want to write to my sister, will you help me, Jani?"

As Jani began typing she assured Max he could be absolutely honest with her. Max wished he could write the letters in private by himself as he went into a dream state and pretended that he was.

> To Tweet,
>
> I love you, Tweet. On that long ride from Mexico's forestlands in the back of an unmarked van driven by an underground bird marketer we had the privilege of being housed next to the toucan. On mountain curves on the way to the international bird

smuggling market you, Tweet, my beloved sister, hung on to the side of the cage that was nearest to him, as if making an attempt to rub feathers with a bird who turned out, I know now, to be one of the winners in the sweepstakes of Pet Bird Life. I didn't care, we were just babies, didn't even have enough sense then to know anything.

We survived just by chance, having never experienced a normal life. We had never had seeds digested, served to us warmly regurgitated from our mother's throat in a way that would have been in harmony with nature. But nevertheless, we were able to hang on to our lives bravely.

The toucan commanded respect just by his posture. Without thinking, you gravitated to his side looking for protection. You gazed at him with your unknowing eyes, maybe not comprehending that he was not the one who was your brother, the one that would have cut off his feathers for you. Oh, Tweet, how I wish I could have protected you. How I wish I could have matured overnight and grown flight feathers and tucked you into my breast and flown us off to find others of our species, brothers and sisters of an extended family that we could perch with in a natural breeze.

I am so sorry my first thought was for my own survival, hoping for more downy feathers to ward off my cold, more pablum to feed my stomach, less joggling on the road. I am sorry I did not convey this to you, Tweet, but maybe I did, I only know that I hate that toucan. He is a nothing, yet I heard he was flown to the US, slickness itself, to live in posh places I can only imagine, admired for his big bones, weighty beak, and because his colors look good together.

Letter to Tweet

My anger festers, because I lost you, because of the irreversible thrust of what our life turned out to be. I held your sweet memory to the down in my breast and the vision of your feathers I still hold dear, yet I must release them to the flow of what once was if I am ever to build a life for myself, here, in these strange waters on an island surrounded by weaving studios and artists, and the strange ideas and values of human kind.

I have been granted a position as Director of Publicity at Aztec Art Gallery, a unique position to be granted to a humble bird. I try to keep frustration under feathers but last night I dreamt of mother. Her wings flapped as she descended from the rainclouds with my breakfast. I woke up and let out one loud squawk in protest of my being here, sitting on a ceramic tile countertop, facing an ancient loom, enslaved in captivity. To my distress, my patrona, Jani, who thinks she owns me, woke from her sleep and came running.

"Good grief my birdie poo, everything is all right, I am right here with you!" she exclaimed, removing the striped serape that kept me warm at night.

How insulting! How can I expect to hang onto my masculinity in a situation like this? I turned my tail to her and perched facing the near wall, my beak in line with its corner.

She has the habit of collecting cats whose noses I always have to scratch. Now why would a person with a parrot want to collect cats? I can only cope with this by thinking about that toucan, about how he is probably also penned in a cage, in a rage, but may not have the upside that I do.

53

Letter to Tweet

Please forgive me Tweet, for I think I will become human, and from that I can never return. It is a one way journey. You see, I have come to love them because they love me and because you are not here and maybe have ceased to be.

Your one and only brother, now known as Max Bird
P.S. I will see you in eternity.

"You have got to be kidding me!" Francisco protested after Max showed him the letter the following morning. "I thought you and Jani were writing something of importance, but this letter is just a lot of whining!"

"*What?*" Max squawked. He had not expected that anyone would say bad things about writing to a lost sister. Francisco's harsh opinion hurt.

"You are acting like a gringo," Francisco went on as he stretched out one leg macho style and planted his foot on the floor for emphasis, "And your letter is not even written in Spanish!" Are you from north of the border? Why didn't you ask *me* to help you? Am I now the only Mexican in this house?"

"You are? I mean, you're not? Max stuttered, wiping a tear from his eye. "But you don't suffer over your past like Jani and I do, you are so matter-of -fact."

"I do suffer, Max, but I don't wallow in it! I suffer when there is nothing to eat. I suffer when I am in pain and when I lose someone I love. I do not suffer from guilt. Guilt is something people create for themselves when there is no justifiable suffering," Francisco told Max.

"But don't you ever feel sorry?"

"Of course, lots of times. When I do something that is not right, I am sorry. I try not to do the same thing again, and then... that is it, case closed. But guilt? Guilt is not normal for a Mexican; we don't have time for it."

"Jani said that we needed to face up to the truth. That's what I was doing. I was *not* whining, Francisco."

"Okay, I guess I was wrong. I am sorry I jumped on you, maybe I felt a little...jealous, but I am angry that you slammed Jani like you did in that letter. You need to tell her that you are sorry for calling her your 'patrona,' sorry that you had her type up those nasty things you said about her...twerping away on her shoulder as she typed it up! You should feel ashamed right now, that's how you should feel, Max. Your behavior... the behavior of *both* you and Jani is unbelievable! If all of us were at liberty to speak the truth whenever it appeared, there would be nothing but misery in this life. Do you understand what I am saying?"

"Yes...I do, Maestro," Max replied, feeling bruised, realizing what an unjust thing he had done to Jani, thinking that Francisco was right about not always telling the truth, yet knowing that dishonesty would not fix the wrong he had done.

"But Jani said the truth would bite you if you denied it."

"Knowing the truth and wanting to hear it are two different things. Do you always have to ask so many questions? Look, Max, you live the human life, that's fine...and you choose to identify with the gringos...that's fine too...but you must remember that they have time to create ways to make life miserable."

"I must tell Jani that maybe a gallery director is not who I am. Actually, I'm police officer material."

"Good grief, Max, that is ridiculous. What would the police department do with a bird?"

"A lot, Maestro. I have superior hearing and as far as I know I am the only bird that talks. Who else can give them the information they need to go after those wild bird marketers who held Tweet and me captive? How can I live this life with you and feel right about it, when they continue to sell birds into slavery while I do nothing to help stop it?"

"It is late and Jani is still in bed ... and I am afraid you have done more damage to her than you realize. That is what you *should* be thinking about!"

"I am sorry I said those bad things about Jani, Francisco. I wasn't thinking. How can I put things back the way they were?"

"You can't, Max; all you can do is repair some of the damage."

Jani sat in the child's chair as instructed at a weaver's studio in Jocotepec. "But we LOVE to have women visit us in our studios," Max said

9
Señora in Blue Linen

When Max asked Jani to help him write a letter to Tweet she had not expected to be judged so harshly in it. The following morning when they exchanged greetings, something had changed.

"Good morning, boss," Max cheeped with his usual good humor."

Jani gave her usual reply. "Good morning, Max, and how are you this morning?"

It was the end syllable on the last word that disturbed Max. The way the "ing" in *morning* dropped an octave instead of lifting. He knew her heart was sad.

Jani had planned on writing a book, an inspiring book about their life. She wanted it to be a book full of hope and possibilities. Maybe she was too close to Max Bird and Francisco who would be her main characters. She believed in the strength of truth, that the value of truth surpassed that of momentary hurt, that a foundation must be free of air bubbles and termite damage, be rock hard and yet flexible, especially in building a foundation strong enough to withstand sometimes brutal exterior forces, but she didn't like it when she was judged harshly. Jani wished Max had not been *so* truthful in his assessment of his life with her. She wished to be thought of as perfect as she herself believed. Her hurt stung deep.

Jani stayed upstairs, keeping her pain securely wrapped in the folds of her old robe. She did not want to face the happenings of this day; she needed to be alone.

Francisco and Max were in the street at the front of their gallery in a flurry of activity arranging balloons to string across their service road. They were doing it as a surprise for Jani.

Francisco remembered he had not given Max his morning bird seed. "I'm sorry, Max," he said. "I forgot to feed you. I'll run in and bring out your breakfast."

"Just put the seeds next to my cage, I'll eat them later. Thanks, Maestro."

Max and Francisco wanted this to be a day to show Jani that they also had the power to get things done. They wanted to show her they could help at the gallery without being asked. They wanted to make her proud of them, to make her feel that she was not alone.

As they were outside stringing up balloons, Jani was upstairs fuming. How could she be so stupid as to type up a letter for an ungrateful bird? Why should she feed him sunflower seeds and not chicken feed? She saw no reason Francisco could not hang out the tapestries without being told. Why was it, she mistakenly thought, he was unable to do anything unless specifically asked?

Jani took comfort in her bathrobe, the one her sister brought her from Detroit 10 years before. It was grossly oversized, red with white snowflakes, acrylic, and just the right weight not to crowd the washing machine. White cat

60

hairs could not be seen on it; big cuffs on the arms when folded down concealed her fingertips and could be used as hot pads. The melted scorched parts at the end of those cuffs were testimony to many good breakfasts past. In the summer it concealed her bare body, in the winter the hooded sweatshirt and warm boots she wore under it were hidden from view. Her attachment to the bathrobe was the real reason she did not nag Francisco to make the place look like it was actually open. On days like this, when she assumed Francisco would be waiting for her instruction, she had the opportunity to pretend she was a recluse where nothing need concern her.

Jani put a newspaper on the footstool in front of her recliner and propped up her dirty feet, pleased with the thought she had the freedom to weed in the garden in her bare feet and that there was nobody who could tell her to clean them. There was no reason for her to wash, get dressed, or comb her hair since, she thought, nobody would be coming into their place.

When she did not tell Francisco to open the doors, she could presume to have privacy. It was only occasionally that Francisco opened the door without telling her and she was caught in her bathrobe. In that case it was to her advantage that she could blame Francisco for not reminding her that the studio was open.

On that day, when it was time to open the gallery, Max and Francisco felt empowered. They were so satisfied with themselves. Francisco decided to open the gallery without being told.

"Look at the balloons bouncing around and our signs out on the street, Max! The front of our studios now looks *really* alive! Why haven't we done this before? I am sure Jani will be pleased when she sees them!"

"Let's go up right now and get her so she can see what we have done!" Max said.

"It is better we wait until she is ready to come down," Francisco replied.

Francisco folded back the outside metal door. It was once a garage entrance, now vertically sliced and fitted to neatly reveal the entrance to their place. He walked to his studio behind the courtyard and began weaving.

Max sat on his birdcage munching sunflower seeds. He loved it when the front doors were propped open wide so he could feel the breeze as it came in from the street to ruffle his feathers. He knew how to handle being in charge. He elevated his plumes, stretching himself out full length while clutching the cage's round top, hanging onto its bars. He faced the entrance so that anyone walking along outside could look in and see him.

Max had a way of what might be called "flapping elbows." His wingtips folded back and tucked up under his breast sockets while flexing his shoulders in a macho posture that said he was in charge. There was a flip side to this mannerism. It made him look as if he were a bird in a cartoon hopelessly trying to lift off, impeded by the dirigible of his cage. Even so, it could be seen that he was a credit to his species.

The "Do Not Let the Turtle Out" sign that was hanging on the door handle fell onto the señora's foot as she entered.

Max Bird squawked out, "Are you okay?"

The well-dressed woman, elegant in a blouse of blue linen, spun around turning her back to Max, pretending to look through the racks of tapestries hanging in the storefront.

She did not want to be caught looking ridiculous by answering a parrot.

He spoke to her again. "Beautiful day!" (Prickles, he thought, I sure hope her foot is okay.)

The señora continued looking at the tapestries in a daze. Was she losing her mind? That couldn't possibly be a bird talking to her.

"Just call me Max," he squawked... "I am the public relations director here at Aztec Studios."

It took a few more minutes before she had the nerve to look his way again. She turned around to face him. He continued speaking.

"We do all of the work here ourselves. The weavings are wonderful, don't you agree?"

She did not answer him at first, only studied him closely. After glancing around to see if there was anyone within earshot, she asked, "Was that you speaking?"

"Yes, it was me, Max Bird of Aztec Studios! Each weaving is original. They were inspired by the prehispanic peoples of ancient Mexico."

"Oh?" the woman nervously replied.

"They were designed by a famous artist from Chicago and the Maestro Francisco Urzúa who is the finest weaver in all Jalisco! They live here with me," Max said.

She stepped up closer to him. "They do?" She adjusted her glasses.

"You will love our place!"

"I will?" the señora, in doubt, replied.

"You don't mind if I perch up on your shoulder do you? I'll take you on our tour. We need your legs to help us along."

To the señora's amazement, before she had a chance to protest, Max hopped up on her shoulder, his talons gently clutching onto her lovely blouse. She silently marched straight ahead through the courtyard without looking right or left, as Max pointed one wing sharply ahead. Max was anxious for the señora to see Maestro Francisco weaving a tapestry.

Max hopped onto the Maestro's almost room-sized loom as they entered. The señora froze inside the doorway, still as a statue. Francisco motioned to her, inviting her to sit down. The señora collapsed into the loveseat facing the foot of the loom. She welcomed its refuge, heaving a sigh of relief, as she sank into it softly.

Francisco was weaving with an easy rhythm as he followed the myriad of dots traced in India ink on the warp stretched out before him. Jani's original pattern hung from strings at the top of the loom, dangling inches away from his concentrated brow. His fingers flew with incredible dexterity as he manipulated spools of different colors to make the design grow across the weft of the loom while he kept an eye on the paper pattern hanging above.

The señora watched Francisco as his body swayed in an easy rhythm in sync with his two-harness loom. He beat the warp down with a comb every few rows, pulling the ancient loom's swinging arm toward him to pack the weft evenly, his feet pumping up and down on the floor pedals as if it were a bicycle. The señora lapsed into a state euphoria. Her body began to move with the cadence of the loom. She lost track of time and strangely began thinking of the ocean, of the tides going in and out.

As she drifted off into a dream world, Max realized he was losing his customer. He knew he had to take action. In his effort to get her attention he hopped onto Francisco's

64

arm, and with his beak attempted to help the Maestro pull wool through the rows of warp.

"See this," Max called out, trying to regain her attention. "We are the only weavers in all of Jalisco that can weave this fast. Isn't that true, Maestro?"

Francisco nodded, embarrassed by Max's bragging. "Do you see this wool, Señora?" Max asked, grabbing a strand in his beak. "We dyed it by hand. It is guaranteed not to fade. You do like wool don't you? All of those from north of the border like wool. Want to smell it?" The woman shook her head back and forth.

"*NO?* But gringos *all* want to smell it! It is not the same wool used in rugs made in Oaxaca. They raise a different kind of sheep, Chira? Shira?"

"*Hey, Señora, are you falling asleep?* C'mon, I'll hop back up on your shoulder and show you the gallery. You can see our new floodlights, they just cost us a bundle."

The señora was not taken with as much surprise when Max hopped onto her shoulder a second time... that was, not until he accidentally eliminated on her.

"Oh, dear Lord!" she screamed. "That dirty creature pooped on my shoulder. Help! Get him off of me. Help, help!" she cried out hysterically, shaking her shoulder to dislodge Max as he held on more tightly in fear of falling head first onto floor.

Jani heard the screams and came running down the stairs. She untangled Max, who had his deformed talon innocently trapped under the shoulder strap of the woman's brassier. She took the señora by the hand and returned her to the loveseat. The woman sat back down next to Francisco who had left his loom and now sat holding his head in distress. With his short square stature and round face, the color of

65

burnished honey, there was no question about his Mayan heritage. He looked into the señora's face with compassion, his eyes avoiding her soiled shoulder.

Max was sitting on the arm of the settee, head hung in shame. When he looked up he was a little more than a beak away from the mess he had made on her. He stared at it in fixation, like he was in a state of shock.

Francisco understood that Max's voiding on the señora was devastating to her. He sensed that she felt her own worth had been lessened by it. Avoiding Max's *mistake* and careful not to disturb her silver tipped hair, he put his arm around her. The señora could not believe she would let a strange man touch her like that, yet she felt comforted and did not want him to take his warm hand from her shoulder. Francisco felt tender towards aging women. He saw in them a feeling of desperation as they hung onto their independence with a pride that belied the fact that there was really no other choice.

"I am sorry about what happened to you," Francisco told the señora. "Max is so full of shame. It was really *my* fault the accident happened. I forgot to feed him his breakfast at the usual time. If I had, the accident would not have happened."

"Think about how lucky you are," Francisco continued, "Your eyes, Señora, are lovely, the same blue as your blouse, and your hair is like silver." Tears began to roll down her face. She sobbed as Francisco held her. "It has been a long time since anyone held me," she said.

Max Bird wished he was anywhere but here, in this place, at this moment. The only option he saw to reclaim his self-respect was to make a dignified apology. With an awkwardness that made him appear insincere, he addressed the señora.

Señora in Blue Linen

"I inadvertently had an accident on your shoulder," Max said, startling the woman and destroying her mellow mood. Francisco began to feel awkward sitting with his arm still around the señora. When he withdrew his arm the señora felt he was withdrawing his support of her as well.

Max knew his approach to the señora had not turned out right. As his good fore-claw dug into an imaginary flea, he gathered the courage to address her one more time. Nervously twisting his beak this way and that, he irritatingly screeched in almost undecipherable words, "I can assure you, Señora, it will not happen again." Then in a squawk that vibrated in their eardrums he blurted, *"I AM SORRY!"*

"SORRY!" the señora wailed in such close proximity that he gasped from the smell of Listerine on her breath. "You are a bird! You know nothing about sorry! This blouse is made of the finest linen. A dressmaker designed it for me in a little shop in France. It is from Paris, do you hear me, Paris!" she hissed.

Max was trembling. His eyes whirled in and out in alarm. She was nose to beak with him. "Who is Paris?" Max meekly inquired.

The señora looked down at Jani's dirty feet in plastic thongs. Jani stood before her scrutiny in humiliation. She was painfully aware of her uncared for fingernails, of her robe's scorched cuffs, of dirt caked between her toes. She gripped the front of her robe whose zipper had long ago broken. Woman to woman Jani looked the señora square in the eye but could think of nothing to say. Francisco saw her plight and pointed to the bathroom door.

Jani sat on the toilet seat and looked at her feet. They were even worse than she had thought. She looked at herself in the mirror. White roots peered out from under her maroon hair. She regretted having decided to go from red to white,

67

as in-between she looked like a drab clown. Entering the bedroom she tossed her robe over a hook and put on fresh jeans and a tee shirt. She discarded the idea of covering her wiped off, but still dirty, feet with shoes. The woman's knowledge of what was under them would be even more shameful than the exposed truth.,

Francisco took some rags and cleaning fluid out of the cupboard. The señora was breathlessly still as Francisco lifted the mess off her once pristine blouse. With cleaning fluid he rubbed back and forth on the señora's shoulder until the soiled spot disappeared. "Maximo," Francisco called. "Look at the señora, she is as good as new!"

The señora looked over and saw Max trembling. She took pity on him. "I would like to see your gallery, if you would show me," she asked Max in an act of kindness.

When Jani returned, the señora was listening to Max give a lecture from the top of a display table. She tiptoed by them and went to join Francisco who was weaving. She looked tired. "Your eyes are beautiful too, Jani," Francisco said. "They are bluer than the sky."

"Look over there...under spotlights number one and two," Max was telling the señora. "Those are paintings of children performing Dance of the Old Men on Mezcala's plaza. You were looking at weavings of them when you first came in the front door... the crosses on their aprons show it is Day of the Cross, your Labor Day... and under spotlights number three and four are paintings of students that Jani left behind in Detroit...you would not be interested in them, they are leftovers." Max fluttered in excitement going on to describe all of Jani's paintings as the señora shifted her weight from one foot to the other.

68

Señora in Blue Linen

"And now we come to the weavings. In an intricate row Francisco will have as many as 25 spools going. The spools were wound using an old bicycle rim, on our spinning wheel over there," Max pointed. "The knowledge of how one material will weave into another without warping, and the amount of tension it can withstand, is like geometry but not the kind you would learn in school. It's a skill you need to be born with. Weaving on this type of loom is a man's job. Actually, most weavers don't welcome women near their looms. They are told to sit in the child's chair beside the loom when they enter. Of course, that is an old fashioned idea. We love women who watch us weave here at Aztec Studios!"

"But why is it a man's job?" she asked.

"Because, you see, it is done by standing up and pushing on pedals. The pedals are stiff. It is a lot of work to keep them going up and down all day. And this is done with the weaver, arms stretched out as far as they will go, leaning over the part he has finished weaving. A woman doesn't have enough muscles in her back to do this. That is why it is a man's job, Señora!"

"That is interesting, but I must...."

"Now over there..." Max went on, "are original tapestries inspired by the Maya, and Jani's collages inspired by the Aztec culture...."

Three quarters of an hour had gone by. With a last throw of the shuttle, Francisco came out from behind the loom. Entering the gallery, he picked up Max and placed him up high on a rack of tapestries.

"What do you think you're doing," Max squawked. "I was giving a lecture. I am the public relations director in this gallery!"

69

Señora in Blue Linen

Francisco, with his hands on his hips stared at Max.

"Okay, I'll zip my lip, just get me off of here," Max implored, and flapping his wings Max landed on Francisco's shoulder.

"Perhaps I can find a place for one of your tapestries in my guest house when I return next season," the señora said. "But now I need to be on my way. Oh, there is so much for me to do! I need to give my maid her severance pay. She wanted $100 pesos (10 dollars) a week to come check on my house. Can you imagine that? A friend at church offered to do it for me for nothing, as a kindness to another Christian in need."

"Where's your church? I need to join," Jani remarked. Francisco, afraid Jani would make another snide comment tapped her arm. The señora paid no attention.

"I never get to the end of paying for everything. And my hand brushed against the side of your settee as I sat down. The glue on my new fingernails was not quite dry. If you could find my nail I would feel *so* relieved!"

Max dug his beak into the settee and retrieved the pink nail, "Max Bird at your service!" he said.

Francisco had placed the nail in his up-turned palm. He handed it to the señora as if it was an offering. Plucking the nail out of his hand, the señora replaced it with a 10 peso coin.

The three of them walked the señora to the door. Max first waved with one wing, then the other. "We have more tapestries, perfect for your casita. Come back to see us. We do special orrrrders...just for youuuu ...." he screeched as the woman in blue linen drove off in her Mercedes Benz.

Francisco lived in an abandoned silver mine way up on a
mountain. Jani and Teo brought him food.

10
Balloons in Apology

Jani, Francisco, and Max stood in the wake of the Mercedes' dust as the woman in blue linen drove off down the cobblestone service drive, her arm trailing out the window as she shouted, "Ta ta!" Francisco stood beside Jani like a squat Indian, arms folded across his chest, a disgruntled Max Bird on his shoulder.

"I should have snatched that woman's fake nail and stomped on it," Jani thought, "ground it into the floor. For a moment I even felt sorry for that woman, could sense her pain, even identify with it, then I had to witness her putting a ten peso coin in Francisco's palm for the nail Max had retrieved with all of his heart, as if Francisco were a beggar. But, how did I get stuck with a bird, anyway, one that would hop on a woman's shoulder unasked, then crap on it? Isn't that just my fate, cleaning up after a bird? Sometimes I wish I could give him away."

Jani knew the time had long past that she could part with Francisco, or Max, that whatever fate had in store for them was to be. They had taken over her heart, had become part of who she was, a part that if she was free to change she would choose to keep, but still, she wondered, "Have I made a cage, a beautiful Mexican cage where I now live trapped by my own devotions?"

It wasn't her that got Max out of trouble this time, it was Francisco, Jani realized. She felt threatened at the thought of a man in the household being her equal. "I felt safer when I carried Francisco around like he was an egg, ready to hatch, after he had been fighting unknown demons on the plaza, when he had to be taken to live in Teo's abandoned silver mine way up on the mountain and we brought him food.

How many years have gone by since I finally agreed to adopt Francisco, bring him into my home? Four or five? A time when he was confused and helpless. Could he discover where I am most vulnerable, use it against me, after I came all this way into central Mexico in an effort to be free? How could I think he would do such a terrible thing? Is it time to learn to trust? But trusting is reckless. Max is perched testimony to that. With one glance at Max and Francisco, still standing out in the street, she spun around and ran to the comfort of her bed.

Francisco opened Jani's bedroom door a crack. He and Max stuck their heads in. "I wish your journal writing never happened, Max, now shut the door and leave me alone!" Jani ordered.

Max let out a chirp that sounded a little like a wail as he listened to the muffled sounds of Jani crying.

"Spent words cannot be retrieved, Max," Francisco told him. It is like trying to retrieve a moment in time. More words do not heal, only actions can do that."

"But I *have* to go in and tell Jani I take my words back, Maestro, I just have to! We have to make her come out and look at the balloons. The gallery in front is so beautiful now, Maestro, but she stayed upstairs, didn't look outside, and then when we saw the señora off, Jani still didn't look."

74

Balloons in Apology

"Looking at something and seeing it are two different things, Maximo. Take this as a lesson to be more careful with your words."

"But humans use negative words all of the time. "

"That is one of the bad parts about being human, Max."

"But that is a part I can avoid because I am part bird. Right?"

Max was the first to wake up the following day. He used this private time for his morning ritual. As if reciting the rosary he repeated the total recollection of sounds he made when he was once pure parrot, squawking out about 70 human words, meowing cats, dogs barking, chickens squawking and the welding that went on in the commercial business next door. He perversely kept a stash of peanuts hidden and would periodically stop chanting and take a chomp out of one of their shells and spit it out into the courtyard. He would then save the whole peanut to snack on mid-morning.

On this morning as he recited, however, he violently ripped at the whole peanuts and threw bits of them out along with the shell and cursed while doing it. Jani's sadness weighed heavily on him.

"Let's think up a plan of action, maybe a very special breakfast to cheer Jani up, Max. I could make eggs just the way she likes them."

"And bacon, she just loves bacon, Maestro. We can run down to the store and buy a whole kilo, boy will that fill her up... and I can flap my wings and pretend I am flying and we can buy fresh sunflower seeds and it wouldn't hurt to get some more peanuts. I am running low on peanuts."

"Buying the bacon will be enough, Max."

75

Balloons in Apology

Jani hardly had the will to get out of bed the next morning. She felt isolated, could not see without her glasses, could not remember where she left them, her hearing aids were defective... but her sense of smell was not. She wanted to be alone yet the mouth-watering whiff of bacon frying told her she was not. She sniffed its delectable goodness. The thought of savoring its smoky flavor, biting into its crispness, chewing on its rind, gnawing on a hunk of fat, made her sit up in bed. She was sure she had been a dog in one of her past lives. The smell seemed to be coming closer. She put on her robe and then her shoes, which carried her into the gallery, a step outside of her bedroom door.

Max was nervously scraping his hooked upper beak over his lower one in anticipation of putting the words he said about Jani in his journal behind him. He perched atop an inverted soup bowl sitting on Francisco's lap. The bowl was covering a plateful of fresh bacon and two eggs, over easy. Francisco was holding a helium filled balloon on which he had written "*TE QUIERO MUCHO*" with a magic marker.

When Jani walked into the room Max stopped grinding and impulsively grabbed the balloon away from Francisco. He began bobbing his head back and forth as if it was a windshield wiper while clutching onto its string, giving the balloon the effect of a flag waving. Jani was smitten. There they were, Max and Francisco, her life's destiny, in their entire glorious splendor. They bowed their heads in homage to Jani, and then Francisco winked at Max. Finally they had done *exactly* the right thing.

"Later we have another surprise for you... outside!" Max shouted. Jani was so touched with the sentiment scrawled on the balloon she did not hear him.

76

Balloons in Apology

"And a helium filled balloon!" Jani raved. "What a wonderful beginning to a new chapter in our lives. And where did you get the balloon?"

"At the party store in Ajijic," Max boasted while Francisco tugged at Max's pin feathers, trying to get him to shut his beak.

"Ajijic? Francisco took you all the way to Ajijic? Today?"

"Nope, yesterday, while you were asleep. I had to hang onto Francisco's shirt with all my might. He pedaled his bicycle like a speedway driver on the shoulder of the highway with *lots* of traffic whizzing along with us. And, when we went downhill we raced cars and I flapped my wings furiously. As we flew down the highway, the passengers inside waved at us through the windows and once we rode alongside a pickup truck whose bed was filled with workers and they tossed me a tortilla and when I caught it they all cheered. I tell you, Jefita, yesterday was such a beautiful day!"

Jani was flabbergasted by this information. She was alarmed fearing for Max's safety, yet chose not to make into a negative a magical time such as this.

"Do you forgive me for those bad things I said about you in my journal?" Max pleaded. "Please forgive me. Will you help me write in it again, Jefita?"

"How could I not forgive you, my bird? How could I not forgive a heart as pure as yours? Later we will think of someone else, someone outside of our little family, to help you with your journal. For now let's celebrate our new beginning. I am starving and the bacon is getting cold," Jani said.

Taking the plate off Francisco's knees she placed it on the work table in the adjoining room and pulled up a chair. Max and Francisco stood beside Jani benevolently looking down upon her as she ate. "Mmm...," she said, blissfully munching on her breakfast.

Max dug his talons into the feathers on his forehead as he passed the time waiting for Jani to finish eating. He wished she would hurry up. He could visualize the balloons outside tossing around in the breeze; he just knew the sight of them would make her *very* happy.

"Do you like the eggs?" Francisco inquired.

"Don't interrupt her eating. It is slowing her down," Max said out of turn.

Francisco left to unbolt the security doors that hid the gallery's façade at night. He opened the glass front door and stepped out into the street.

"Are you almost done? You *are* almost done, aren't you, Jefita?" Max implored. "Let's go, let's go, let's go outside, Francisco is already out there! You can carry that last piece of bacon with you!"

Max clapped his wing struts as he wobbled down the garden walk. Jani followed him, still chewing. Elliot strutted behind her, and Isabella Cat tagged behind him, one ear flattened in mild irritation for having been woken from her nap.

The balloons had shriveled during the night. Francisco looked back, watching the others approach. Max reached the door first and looked outside. "Our balloons, what happened to our balloons?" He screeched in disappointment.

"I wish you could have seen how beautiful they were yesterday morning Jani," Francisco told her. The colors were so fresh, and they bounced around in the breeze."

"Francisco spent his birthday money on them, Jefita. We wanted to make you proud of us."

Balloons in Apology

Bursting into a smile, Jani's face took on a radiant glow. "This is a wonderful beginning for a new chapter," she said. "I see what fills my eyes with pleasure and it is not spent balloons. It is your hearts beating full of a glorious color, one not seen before. I am happier than I have ever been in my life, my precious ones," she told Max and Francisco. "A moment like this can more than balance out a whole lifetime of bad history."

"I can be of assistance in capturing the bird traffickers
in Guadalajara," Max told Sergeant García.
"Only I can recognize their van because I was in it!"

11
Police Passion

The two-lane highway beyond their cobblestone service drive could have been the approach to an American tourist town back in the 1940's if it were not for signs in Spanish along the highway. It was the last stretch of road to pass that slow car in front of them, the stretch of road before the speed bumps, where the drivers looked directly ahead, not noticing the blinking OPEN sign on the front of Aztec Studios.

Lake Chapala was the destination for many retired seniors from the United States and Canada aspiring to live the great life. The villages that surround the lake became a home for those that fell in love with Mexico. Those were the souls that Max Bird had dreamed would find them, would buy Jani's paintings and Francisco's hand-woven tapestries.

Max was in a thoughtful mood. "Jani says she is a goose," he remarked. "Now since she adopted you, does that make you a goose, a parrot, a gringo, or something else? Do you wish you were the same color as her? I like my feathers but I dream of having hands, Maestro."

Francisco gave the question some thought before he replied. "I am a weaver, that is who I am. I could never become a bird, Max. Dreams are good, life would be less if we did not have dreams, but it is a mistake to dream of being something that you are not."

"And I am a bird with good moral character, and *I* am brave and fearless and *I* want to become a police officer. Jani said I need to be able to deal with reality, and the reality is I need a better job as we do not sell enough tapestries here."

"But we need you to be our public relations director."

"The police department needs someone like me to help *them* with *their* public relations."

"Sometimes I wonder if we will ever be able to stop clipping your wings, Max!"

Max had just finished taking a nibble from Francisco's carrot stick when a mud spattered police vehicle pulled up in front of them. Sergeant García and his recruit got out. They parked to take advantage of the hose the gardener next door had left running. The recruit held onto a sponge as the sergeant started hosing the vehicle down. Max quivered with excitement, fanning his tail feathers, his eyes aglow.

"Wouldn't it be great to ride around all day in a big truck wearing an impressive uniform that got everybody's respect?" Max twittered. "Wouldn't you love to be a police officer, Maestro?"

"No," Francisco replied, frowning.

"But why not?" Max asked. It would sure be a whole lot better than being a weaver and having to keep this place clean, washing floors that have to be washed again, again and again." Max hopped off Francisco's shoulder and waddled over to the officers.

"Good afternoon, officers," Max said in his gruffest voice, beak pointed into the air at the policemen towering above him. "What a wonderful day to wash a police vehicle. It would look a whole lot more impressive if it was cleaner. Max Bird here, we would be happy to be of assistance," he

82

said, holding out a wing in greeting. The recruit stared at Max standing in the road in front of his feet. The sergeant pretended he wasn't there.

Refusing to be ignored, and determined, Max continued. "Hey, you missed a spot, right there," he pointed, "and another one over by that bang on the fender. Want me to help you? I can send my runner into the house to get some soap. *MAESTRO!*" Max squawked as he pointed a wing at Francisco, hopelessly imitating a drill Sergeant trying to get his troops to fall in line. *"Get the officers some soap!"* The recruit took a swig of coke.

"They say that parrot talks, did you hear him talk?" The sergeant asked his recruit.

"Nunca," The recruit replied, not quite understanding what the sergeant wanted him to say, then, shiftily casting his eyes on the roadway replied, "We are police officers! I don't think we should have let a bird talk to us like we were his buddies though!"

"Please, get the soap for me, Maestro," Max begged in a whisper as he hopped back up on Francisco's shoulder. "I may never get this chance to know real policemen again!"

"Okay, Maxie, but first take your beak away from my eardrum."

Francisco, Max bouncing along on his shoulder, went into the house and brought out soap and window cleaner. He set Max down on the hood of the police truck to supervise. The sergeant stepped aside and let the recruit and Francisco wash the truck, fascinated that a bird could wield enough power to boss two large men.

"I have not been a policeman but I have been known in the past for my valor," Max addressed the Sergeant and the recruit, chest expanded to its full capacity, wings at his side, shoulders strutted up as if he wore stripes on them, chin tucked under salute style. Max was a small but imposing creature perched atop the police truck. To Francisco's surprise Max made the officers a proposition.

"I was captured by criminals, a syndicate of poachers, with first class technological equipment. I escaped and was able to take my sister with me. I am now here to be of assistance to you in capturing these outlaws," Max said, as if reciting a line from a movie.

The officers, taken by surprise, didn't know what to make of Max's offer. Sergeant García, however, became intrigued. He was ready to retire and had been saddled with keeping this young recruit *out of trouble*, as he was the youngest son of the Police Chiefs' favorite sister. He was open to have something, anything, which would break up his day.

"What does valor mean?" The recruit quipped. "Does that mean I have to share my Coke with that bird, Sarge? Is it okay if I answer when he talks? *He does talk, doesn't he?*"

"SURE," the sergeant replied, aware he had been a party to stranger phenomena than this in his career.

The sergeant, concerned that he and the recruit might be seen associating with a parrot, nonetheless decided to sit on the curb and let the afternoon progress. He enjoyed watching Max confidently ordering the recruit around like he was Max's personal assistant.

"I know how you can get to be a sergeant in no time at all," Max eagerly told the recruit. "This is the deal," Max went on, as if in confidence. "You see this van, the color of pewter, will be packed with contraband birds snatched from the wild. The driver will unload their... what they call "*crop*," in front of a mammoth warehouse at the San Juan Market in Guadalajara. *"Only I can recognize that vehicle, because I was in it!"* Max screamed losing his cool in an emotional outburst.

"It is amazing you are here with us now to tell the story, Mister Bird," said Sergeant García.

"We can go to the market on Friday, hide behind a dumpster, and wait for the van. When it arrives you, Sergeant, can pull out your pistol and arrest the driver and let the birds go free. The driver will direct you to the others in the syndicate."

"Not me, son, and I am advising the recruit here not to go either." Max continued as if the sergeant hadn't spoken, this time addressing the recruit.

"There might be a hundred birds inside that van who would think you were God. You would be written up in the newspapers as a hero. I am sure the department would give you a higher position, maybe even the sergeant here's job. No offense to you, Sergeant, but I imagine you are about ready to retire."

"Really?" the recruit replied, enthused, motivated, visions of stripes on his shoulder, but Sergeant García who would love to own a clever bird such as this, had no intention of seeing Max put in danger's way.

"How is it you wound up in the back of that van?" The sergeant asked Max.

"A carload of us birds were gathered up from poachers in small villages scattered around the countryside. We were snatched from our mothers' nests as infants. See my mutilated claws." Max stretched out his right leg and splayed his talons for them to see. His front claw was missing, and the claw in back of his heel, that was necessary for gripping, was broken in half.

"How old were you Max?" the sergeant asked. "Maybe you are not remembering this right. That looks like an injury from a trap, and where *is* your sister?"

85

Police Passion

"I must have had just a little down on my body as I was very cold. I remember my kidnapper's children nursing me with an eye dropper. But, I am not sure about what really happened. Maybe I am wrong, maybe my story is not right," Max guiltily confessed to Sergeant García.

"Then you were too young to be caught in a trap, Mr. Bird. It would have been impossible for you to even be out of the nest if you were that underdeveloped. Now about your sister...."

"She was sold before me, for eight hundred pesos, but it wasn't my fault. I swear it wasn't."

"And why would you think it was Mister Bird?"

"The vendor's big hand reached into our cage and grabbed her. I was startled. Before I realized what had happened there was only me left in that cage! I should have attacked his hand, I should have done something!"

"A bird cannot be expected to fight a grown man, son. It was not your fault!" Max breathed a sigh of relief and felt redeemed by a police official of long standing.

"When we were still babies we were bought from the poacher. His children, who had nursed us, ran after the trafficker's car crying as we drove away. We were taken into a valley somewhere north of Veracruz and stored in a chicken coop. Later we were whisked off across the country to Guadalajara in the van. We were to be unloaded at a warehouse, have bands put on our ankles so we could pass as domestic creatures. I was able to escape, taking my little sister, Peep, with me, saving her from being shipped to the United States and possibly death, maybe even stuffed inside a plastic pipe and loaded into the hold of an airplane," Max said as the others listened in rapt attention.

Police Passion

It was the middle of the day. It was getting hot, real hot, but Max didn't complain as he remained standing on the truck's hot metal roof, as he was a tough bird. Francisco and the recruit joined Sergeant García in the shade admiring the truck's hubcaps, now sparkling clean.

Exhaustion was beginning to overtake Max, his puffed up military stance on the hood of the police vehicle was beginning to wilt. He felt scorched. Given a little more time, he thought, he may not be much more than the truck's missing hood ornament. "Good job, men. This was work well done!" Max said, he thought, appropriately. Then he saluted.

Francisco, the sergeant and the recruit were leaning back against a Jacaranda tree in the soft grass as Max, roasting, looked down on them. He made one more statement before he collapsed. "This vehicle now gives respect to the Chapala Police Department and the citizens of this county for which it serves." Francisco, finally realizing Max's plight, plucked him off the hood before he toppled over, rescuing him, possibly, from an unthinkable fate, but definitely from humiliation.

12

The Bird Traffickers

Sergeant García, who was known for milking the truth out of the hardest criminal, reached over and petted Max. He seemed smaller as the sergeant observed him resting on Francisco's lap, almost too small for a male bird, but his valor made up for that. He observed the bird's fragility under his own tough weathered hand.

"Seems you left a whole lot out of your van story, son," the sergeant told Max. "Did you tell us what *really* happened, or the way you want to remember it?"

Max, lying on Francisco's knees, was dizzy from the heat, yet seized this opportunity for fame. He moved to lie on his back, short legs straight in the air, his crippled foot crossed over his uninjured one, and began to relate his *real* history to the others in a dramatic and articulate voice.

"My sister, Tweet, and I were kept comfortable in a dark chicken coop awaiting our fate. In there with us were a group of twittering canaries, some haughty hook bills splashed with exotic markings, and a toucan."

"Go on with your story, son," the Sergeant said, his voice as smooth as a mother's milk.

The Bird Traffickers

"Occasionally the door would crack open, startling us, as the darkness flooded with light," Max continued, "A strange one-eared man was ushered in. He circled each of our cages, eyes beading in assessment, hands folded behind his back, grunting, sticking up his nose as he paused at our cage. My heart beat wildly with fear. I remember how I strained to hear as our keeper and the wholesaler talked about us outside the door. The effort was futile as I could not hear, but knew from their gestures, the outcome would not be good."

"The van pulled up and parked right next to our chicken coop. It was like a rich man's van and smelled of newness, or was it bleach? An evil man with an aura of detachment came into the coop. You could almost hear our silence as his footsteps deftly padded across the soft dirt floor. He rearranged us as we fluttered wildly in a last ditch effort to escape, transferring us into slick aluminum cages equipped with automatic feeders."

Max stopped for a moment before going on.

"We sped along part of the day and through the night in resigned acceptance of our fate. It was only when the driver stopped to pay a toll that I screamed, "Help, please help!" in an attempt to get us out of there, envisioning being cooked and eaten at the end of our ride. I put everything into those screams but nobody heard. Looking back, we never were eaten, so maybe I overreacted."

"You did the right thing Max. Hollering out was the only option you had," the sergeant told him. Heartened, Max continued with his story.

"Guadalajara was asleep when we arrived, all but the bustling around the old San Juan Market. Caught in a huge traffic jam, in an almost impossible entanglement of vehicles, we wiggled on through. Our driver convinced the

other drivers trying to get through that he had a perishable load, referring to us creatures that chirped."

"I overheard that we were to be taken to a processing station filled with other contraband birds snatched from the wild. The luckiest of us would be put into airplanes and flown to the United States to grace rich persons' homes. The others would be marketed to pet stores here in Mexico. Both of these options looked pretty good, considering just the night before I thought we would be eaten."

"My sister and I, however, were stopped at the entrance of the banding station, putting a halt to our aspirations for the good life."

At this point Max uncrossed his legs and turned over to bury his beak in between Francisco's legs, comforted by the worn khaki that smelled of Francisco.

Tears ran down Francisco's eyes as he heard this story. The sergeant got a lump in his throat, the recruit choked on a Dorito.

"Everything is okay Max, you can continue," the sergeant urged him on, wanting to hear the rest of the story.

Max sobbed, remembering the shame of discovering the worthlessness of his value, the value he once felt he had had. Francisco came to understand why Max needed to brag so much.

"What are those two common parrots doing here?" the man from the warehouse demanded as he spotted my sister and me being unloaded with the others."

"Tweet and I huddled together as we heard our driver's reply. 'But I got ya' the iguana you been wantin' and a real good cash crop of assorted birds here, and just look at that toucan, the biggest I ever did see!"

The Bird Traffickers

"Well, those common parrots are not worth nothin'. Get them out of here," the warehouse supervisor said, his accusing finger pointing at us in disdain."

"There we were, me and my sister, evicted from our cage, just two hunks of trash, and a few ounces of underdeveloped feathers, worth nothing but to be stepped on, unceremoniously dumped into the street."

"Then what happened?" Francisco asked.

"Well, Maestro, that day was to get brighter. A beggar with a soot- filled beard and bare feet suddenly came into our lives. He was standing as if waiting for us as we were dumped beside the curb. He took off his crunched up, sweet scented sombrero, and nested me and my little sister inside of it. As we traveled up the road, with us cradled in his arms, he began humming. Our purple crested heads optimistically bobbed along in unison, almost as if we were on a tour."

"Miraculously, on that day at that very time, the color of the moody sky changed from a dark violet to a glorious orange as the sun rose over the horizon, and to our surprise the beggar began singing us a carol. 'Away in a manger, no crib for a bed, the little lord Jesus lay down his sweet head.'"

Max heaved a bereaved sigh, as Francisco picked him up cradling his body, limp from exhaustion, in his hands. Francisco turned his back to the sergeant and recruit whom he felt had demanded too much from this small bird, and left. He walked through the Aztec Gallery courtyard, past the goldfish, stepped over the turtle, taking Max to his sleeping cage at the foot of his loom in the weaving studio. He tucked Max in, covering the cage with its purple satin throw, a regal setting for the true hero he was.

92

The Bird Traffickers

Sergeant García had felt a twinge of betrayal, even though he knew Max Bird had not made the decision to be coddled by Francisco when he turned his back and walked away. García's seemingly tender uneven brow masked the hardness that had been with him too long, a hardness he wanted to leave behind when he retired.

The sergeant was enthused about Max. He needed Max's enthusiasm for life. He needed him to grace his wife's garden, to keep her company, he needed him to complete his dream of one day opening a private detective agency, one that would have the sleuth to uncover evil wrong doings and expose them.

Max needed to learn the downside of being a police officer. He needed to be informed about the sergeant's plans for the future, plans that could include him.

13
The Golf Cart Woman

"Mornin', Max. Thought I would stop in for a visit," Sergeant García said.

He sidled up to Max casually, as if they had a relationship of long standing. "I think you wanted to hear more about what really goes on in police work. Would you like to learn?"

"Geee—Sergeant García, I would *love* you to teach me about police work! I would just *love* that!" Max said.

"Being a police officer is not a glamorous job. It is not even particularly exciting.   I suspect you have more excitement living in your …uh… *art compound* here than I have on my job. Have you ever noticed that there isn't a parking lot at the police station in Chapala? That is because the policemen who work for this municipality can't afford to buy a car."

"Excuse me, Sergeant," Max interrupted. "In all due respect to you and your profession, that's not what I want to hear about," Max replied in profound disappointment.

"I know you have thoughts of capturing criminals who market birds illegally in the San Juan Market, Max, and I respect you for it, but that could turn out to be very tricky, and you could wind up being the one put in jail. Take my advice, Mr. Max, and do not go, for I know what I am talking about!"

"Would you like to go out with me and see what police work is really all about?" García offered.

"You would do that for *me*, for *Max Bird*, just a common parrot?"

Max sat tall on Francisco's shoulder the following morning as they hopped into the cab of the police truck. "We got a report about an old woman and her Pomeranian thumbing their nose again at the law and good citizens of our community!" The sergeant said, "The chief let her off last time after she practically ran over a citizen on his way to work. We call her the 'Cart Woman.' She thought that since her vehicle was electric she was entitled to use the ciclopista. I taught her differently! The License Bureau drilled a hole in her cart's fiberglass frame to attach the motorcycle plates, but that doesn't stop her! She sailed on by one of our policemen as he tried to stop traffic, almost running him down this morning. Her Pomeranian leaned out of his seat, of course there was no door, snarling and baring his teeth at the officer as the woman laughed and speeded up. The dispatcher said the tassels on her cart's roof swung back and forth and the sparkles from the cart's fiberglass frame shone in the sun as she escaped."

Sergeant García frowned, thinking, "How could *he*, a self-respecting police sergeant, let the likes of *her* humiliate him and the rest of the good citizens in their community?"

"On television policemen go for coffee and donuts in the morning. Do we go for coffee and donuts?" Max asked Sergeant García.

"Of course, Mr. Max. But more important than coffee and donuts is this: we need to ask around to see if anyone has seen that woman before she and her ridiculous dog try to run anybody else down!"

"The Cart Woman's dog took a bite out of my cousin's bicycle tire, *yup*, and he fell off and she tossed him twenty pesos; *yes, she did, boss*," the recruit told the sergeant. The chief says our hands are tied, that we can't arrest her because it would hurt tourism, and city hall won't stand for that. But I saw her on my way to work, Sarge, going down Tempisque. She had a flowered hat strapped on her head with a scarf, and her dog had on a plaid vest!"

The sergeant hadn't driven more than a mile before Max, up front with the sergeant, his eager claws digging into Francisco's shoulder, spotted the woman with his keen eyes, just off the main road, before the others knew there was anything up ahead at all.

"There she is!" Max screeched, pointing his longest feather.

"*Whoop-Whoop- Whoop*, the police siren pounded as Sergeant García enthusiastically picked up speed then braked just behind the Cart Woman. She had seen the pulsating lights menacingly flashing in her rear view mirror. Pulling over she waited for them, eager to challenge the sergeant head on with another confrontation.

"*Buenas dias*, Señora. I see you have a plate on your cart, guess you won't be driving on the ciclopista no more. About your dog, however, I notice he doesn't have a seat belt on. I will have to give you a ticket." The Pomeranian, who sat beside her, bared his teeth at Sergeant García.

"*Oh, no*! That was the wrong thing for that dog to do," Francisco thought.

"Where were you headed, Señora?" the sergeant asked.

"To my bridge club, but I suppose you don't know what that is, so let me explain it to you."

97

The Golf Cart Woman

"Now, Señora, are you insultin' a police officer?" the old sergeant replied, knowing that this was the last time he would stop her, that he was going to put an end to her harassment of policemen and to the citizens of his community. He would make certain that she would never *dare* make a dig at him again.

"No, sir. I just didn't know if you knew what a bridge club was!" she snickered impulsively, even though she sensed that their game had changed, that the sergeant was now playing with a stacked deck.

"Excuse me, Sergeant García," Max interrupted. "The old woman doesn't mean any harm, she just does crazy things. I know you are a kind man, Sergeant García. Can't you let her go with a warning?"

"The Señora knows *exactly* what she is up to, Mister Bird," the Sergeant glared.

The Cart Woman tightened her thin lips even more, as danger warnings instinctively began to creep up the back of her neck. "How about a tip? Say…$500 pesos?" she offered.

"Take the money!" Max cried. "That's a lot of money!" he hollered, hoping to spare the crazy old woman.

"I wouldn't take her money if I was a criminal!" the sergeant, on the brink of a total loss of self-control, barked at Max. "She has come here with the intent of running us Mexicans down with her cart, and she will pay the consequence, and that goes for her plaid-vested *companion* too!"

Cupping his wing up next to Francisco's ear, Max nervously twerped, "That dog is like a baby to her. It may be all of the family she has got! What will we do if they try to take it away from her? We can't just can't stand and watch, can we?" Nothing could be heard except the whizzing of cars on the highway in the ensuing moment of silence.

"You should be charged with animal abuse, lady." The sergeant told the Golf Cart Woman sarcastically, "but, I am letting you go. I *am*, however, taking your precious mutt into the animal shelter for his own protection. He looks like a purebred *something* to me; they ought to be able to find him a real good home in no time at all. You exposed that poor, fancy, innocent, dolled- up dog of yours to danger, with no seatbelt on, not even a door to keep him from falling out when he snarls at police officers, and...."

The Cart Woman panicked when she comprehended the full extent of what the sergeant was saying.

"*Nooo*, you can't take my baby away from me," she screamed, clutching her precious animal to her bosom. The dumb recruit impulsively grabbed onto the Pomeranian trying to wrestle it from her grip.

The sergeant turned away. In his emotional state he had foolishly not thought far enough ahead to figure out how either of them could pry the dog away from her. He knew they were headed for a reprimand if this did not quickly come to an end.

The recruit yanked at the dog's hind legs while the woman and her mutt were glued together, chest to breast, both of them crying in a pitiful wail that echoed out into the street. Max felt his heart would break at the sounds of their combined howling. In a rage, remembering the vendor's hand as it reached in to grab Tweet, he flew at the recruit, flapping his wings hard, screeching, *"This is not right, this is just not right! She is just a crazy old woman, let go, let go. That dog may be all she has."*

Max's wings were just a blur between the recruit's yanking arms, the snarl of dog's teeth and the woman's

99

kicking leg. Francisco was afraid Max would have a heart attack and tried to grab him. Feathers were flying as the recruit grabbed for the dog's front leg. It bit him. Blood ran down the front of his new police shirt. He screamed, *"I'll get you for this, you stupid mutt, you can't get away with biting me!"*

Max's beak tore into the recruit's shirt with a rapidity that was amazing, ripping it open, exposing the recruit's flesh. When Max saw blood on his feathers he yanked even more, adrenaline surging, until the police shirt was in ribbons. The señora's wails became more tormented as she continued screaming, "My baby, don't take my baby."

Outraged drivers slowed down and began tooting their horns in indignation of the brutal sight. Traffic began to pile up on the highway.

"Let go of the dog, you dumb ass! Halt, Recruit! Do you hear me? Halt!" the sergeant ordered. The old woman and her dog ran toward their cart.

The Pomeranian's paws were wrapped around the Cart Woman's neck as she drove away. She held onto him with one arm, as if he were a Teddy Bear, steering the silent electric cart into oncoming traffic that swerved to avoid her. The cart woman's hat became untied and as she picked up speed the wind caught it. In her panic she was probably unaware that it had left her head. It floated in the air before settling down on the shoulder of the road.

The sergeant ordered the recruit into the police vehicle and they headed down a side road. Sergeant García thought of himself as an example of doing what was right, and he wanted to continue doing that when he retired. Max's ears could pick up conversation blocks away. But Max needn't be a block away, he could perch practically beside those that needed to be apprehended in the name of justice, to gather evidence of their wrongdoing, and Max was of good character, like the sergeant himself, and he could be trusted.

"Why didn't you throw that bird in the slammer? A bird that would attack a police officer should not be walking around free, should he Sarge, should he?" the recruit yammered.

"Do you want us to be the laughing stock of the police department, is that what you want?" García who would have liked to forget the golf cart incident, replied.

Francisco held onto Max Bird, feathers askew, exhausted, his adrenaline fading. They sat beside the road until Max stopped shaking before making the short walk home. *"I feel like reality has slapped me in the face,"* Max squawked.

How strange the sergeant did not at least reprimand Max, and that when they left they drove away from town, and *very* strange a police sergeant would take such a big interest in such a little bird, Francisco thought. A little girl ran by them clutching onto the Cart Woman's hat, its ribbons flying, two other girls laughing and running in pursuit.

Sergeant García came to "visit" Max.
Jani and Francisco warily hovered over the loom,
pretending to realign a weaving,
staying in close proximity to watch over Max.

14

Freedom in Corn Tassels

A person with super perception drifting in a helium balloon over Lake Chapala might look down through the layers of Aztec Studios and see a bird and two humans living out their life in an unusual space shaped like a railway siding. Its rooms were not unlike that of a line of arty cabooses… or maybe brightly painted boxcar cages left behind from a Mexican circus, beginning to be overtaken by leafy tropical plants and dripping flowers, the creatures they once held within, now free. This space held, deep in the interior, the concern the two humans inside had for their parrot, a treasured family member.

"Max has a lot of ambition," Jani said, arm wrapped around the loom's vertical support, waiting for him to wake up. Francisco balanced his chair on two legs as he listened to Jani. "Max is stressed by all of the adjustments he has had to make. His ability to talk has been almost too much for him!"

"I'm okay," Max twerped, his middle feather sleepily wiping his eye, as he leaned out the open door of his cage and gave the Maestro's hand a nudge. Francisco soothed the feathers on Max's violet crested head.

Sergeant García was waiting for the gallery to open. He was wearing a sport shirt and blue jeans, but Jani recognized him when she opened the metal doors that secured their property at night.

"Good morning, Sergeant, I'm Jani," she said, and reached out and shook his hand. "Are you here to see Max? He is in his cage in the courtyard. I will show you in." The sergeant resented the abrupt way she shook his hand, the way she walked off.

"You could have been arrested for obstructing justice yesterday, Max. My inexperienced recruit could press charges, but he won't because I told him not to."

"Thank you Sergeant," Max replied.

"I was thinking I would like to go into business when I retire, Max. Maybe open up a private detective agency. Actually I could use a bird like you, with ears that could hear from a great distance."

"...and I speak English!" Max replied.

"It's an unlikely family you have here, Max," the sergeant said looking around, "very unlikely."

Jani and Francisco could not concentrate on straightening out the weaving that had gotten out of alignment, but hovered over the loom as they wanted to stay in close proximity to Max. They could see the facial expressions of Sergeant García from where they stood and could tell his intent on visiting Max was not in just passing the time of day.

"I think I had better go out and see what the sergeant is talking about to Max," Francisco told Jani.

"Maybe we are overprotective, Francisco. We need to have more confidence in Max. It is time he comes to some of his own conclusions, regardless of...'whatever.' Let's leave him to his privacy."

Freedom in Corn Tassels

The sergeant stared at Maria, the turtle who was lounging beside their 'pond.' "That is an illegal turtle," the sergeant pointed. "It is covered under Mexico's wildlife protection laws!"

"Do we need to get a license for her, Sarge?" Max innocently asked.

"I came here as a friend, Max. I am not on duty all of the time, still I must tell you that holding a wild creature hostage is not right!"

"...and what about me?" Max thought out loud. "I was a wild creature once."

"Yes, and what about you?"

Max became aware of the narrow spacing of the bars on his cage, even though they were not at all constraining, as his cage had no door. Nevertheless, for the first time they looked ominous.

"You might think I am a hostage like most parrots, but I am not, Sarge. I am part of this family!" Max replied.

"Yes, I see that!" García said, thinking that maybe he should expand his plan to 'adopt' Max to include the whole family, as he appreciated the well-tended garden and smelled the aroma of chicken soup in the courtyard air.

"I notice the señora provides a pond for the turtle," García went on "and special turtle food is sitting on the steps." Max looked down at the sunflower seeds that Jani had placed in a decorative cup before him. "And someone even wrote *M* in finger nail polish on top of her shell, but we know you didn't do it, there is no fingernail polish on your feathers!" A barely noticeable smirk escaped the sergeant's straight face.

"Are you okay out there, Max?" Francisco hollered out, noticing that the sergeant had taken on a different posture than he had seen before.

"Don't concern yourself with me, Francisco. The sergeant and I are just having a nice visit," Max replied.

"And Francisco!" García remarked, "What a transformation! Why just a few years ago he was a lost person wandering the streets, dressed in crazy clothes, sweeping, continually sweeping with a broken broom, mumbling about keeping the plaza beautiful."

"You knew Francisco? I didn't know you knew Francisco."

"All of the old-timers from Ajijic knew *that* family. Sad the village people couldn't help them more when they were dumped out into the street hungry, followed by the half a dozen looms from Francisco's father's weaving factory. "

Max's heart skipped a beat, as he knew what it felt like to be dumped out into the street, and he couldn't really imagine what it felt like to be hungry. He had the urge to throw his arms around Francisco, to tell him he was sorry, but the sergeant didn't notice that Max felt distress.

"There were just too many of them," the sergeant continued. "Thirteen children with a crazy mother and a father who couldn't be reached because he was mining opals in Magdalena. They were outsiders, Max. They should have stayed in their own village on the other side of the lake!" Max realized that he and Jani, as well as Francisco, were 'outsiders.'

"Francisco's father, Teo, had charm. He was a man who liked to please everyone. (Jani said he was ingratiating.) He always had a friendly wave, was enthusiastic about others' good fortune, and was generous to friends and strangers in hard times, so he was liked by everybody. Francisco's mother was from the Yucatan; she had that Mayan look, the round face, the short square body, and wore her hair back in

106

a braid down to her waist. She loved childbirth, believed being pregnant was holy; each new life she bore she believed was a gift to her from God. She spent her days sitting in the back church pews with her babies, and the janitor from the church of San Francisco de Asis had to kick her and her babies out after he finished cleaning at night. "

"Is that why she named Francisco, Francisco?" Max asked.

"Maybe, I don't know Max. Anyway, she was an angry woman when she was not in church... and she was jealous and fierce, very fierce and dangerous when she got ahold of a pistol, which she did ever few years. She would put on a sombrero and serape as disguise, hunt down and shoot at women she thought were 'coming on' to Teo. I was just a rookie. We would arrest her, of course, and put her in jail, but there was no one to care for her thirteen children and Teo would beg us to let her out so she could nurse their babies."

"Teo came home from the mines to help his wife with the birth of a new life only to find his family on the street, his looms and all of the family's possessions gone. There was one cloth bag of Teo's precious prehispanic artifacts left. When he arrived, Francisco's mother threw it in Teo's face, and the pieces crumbled. She had a baby girl and it died."

"Why did the baby die?" Max asked.

"Nobody knows why," the sergeant replied. "She died in her mother's arms when she was just a few weeks old and Teo's wife was furious. She thought the death of the baby was retribution for the imagined 'bad deeds' she thought Teo had committed against God. Francisco's mother had to be held back from viciously attacking Teo as the funeral procession walked the mile from the church to the cemetery. Their sixteen-year-old daughter's young husband walked along beside the grieving mother, carrying the dead baby in

107

his arms. Keeping a distance, the barely conscious father was being dragged along behind his wife and the dead baby by others who took turns struggling to support him. Their oldest son was Francisco. He was always as serious as he is now, loved school… was in his first year of preparatoria [high school]…too bad about a coyote smuggling him across the border to work in the fields…but I guess there was no other choice, being the others were hungry… and I guess his money did roll in for a couple of years…anyway, Francisco marched in that funeral, with as serious a face as I have ever seen on a youngster, right at his father's side followed by his twelve younger siblings, the older ones taking turns carrying the younger ones, accompanied by many aunts and uncles that helped them along the way."

The sergeant continued, "You are a sinner, a sinner, a sinner," Francisco's mother screamed back at Teo. "She was my gift from God and you killed her!'

"The whole village came, Max. It was a spectacle the intensity of which you would not believe. During the procession the other children were emotionless, like pawns in a game of chess. I suppose they were accustomed to fits of anger and being moved around, but when they watched the baby being taken from their mother's arms, wrapped in a blanket of the purest white, they started screaming in terror and clung to each other. Teo was pulled to the edge of the freshly dug hole. There were so many men surrounding the scene it was impossible to tell how it happened, but it was reported that Teo did throw the first shovelful of dirt on the grave before the other men took turns filling it in, as was the custom."

Freedom in Corn Tassels

Max sat motionless in a state of shock trying to—or maybe trying *not* to—digest the distressing story the sergeant had told him.

Jani looked out and saw the distressed look on Max's face. "This has gone on long enough!" she told Francisco. "I wonder what that old sergeant is filling Max's ears with. I'm going out there and break this up!"

"Sorry I have to shorten your visit, men, but its naptime," Jani informed Max and the sergeant.

"I was just going to leave," the sergeant replied with a false smile but seething inside at her interference. He got sidetracked and had barely broached the subject he had come to talk to Max about.

Max felt embarrassed by the word 'naptime.' Furthermore, Jani's interference reinforced the sergeant's opinion that Max was a 'kept' bird, and even though Max was feeling emotionally drained, he did not want to put an end to what might turn out to be his dream of a lifetime by looking like a wimp.

"I'm not ready for my nap yet, Jani," Max said with a flap. "I want to stay out here and visit. Can you stay a while longer?" he asked the sergeant.

"I see your patrona has you and Francisco fixed up mighty fine, Mister Bird. If I were you I might be satisfied to sacrifice my freedom to live here myself!" the sergeant said after Jani went back inside.

"Excuse me, Sergeant. I would never, ever, call Jani my *patrona.*

"But you are not free, you are a victim of your circumstances, and Janice and Francisco are the facilitators of your incarceration. Now are you getting what I am trying to tell you, Max? "

Max peeped. "I am where I want to be."

109

Freedom in Corn Tassels

"Possibly this *is* a good family, Max. Maybe they just need to be taught a few things," the sergeant replied, knowing he had to back off a little, thinking for a moment that he might benefit by including Jani and Francisco in his plans, but quickly returning to the indoctrination of Max.

"Trust me," García anxiously told Max, feeling he was running out of time, "do not deny yourself the truth or you will be one sorry bird. You are only free within Janice's confines. If you try to escape she will come looking for you, even if where you want to be is not with her. Isn't that right, Mr. Bird? Isn't that proof of what I am trying to tell you?"

Max was puzzled. The old sergeant was acting strange, almost as if his body had been hiding another person inside, and yet it was the same old Sergeant García. He could not disagree with the facts the sergeant had laid out in front of him, facts that were very compelling. Max listened in curiosity as the sergeant went on.

"When you face up to your real situation you will try to escape and I will hear of it and come to your aid. You must listen carefully to what I am going to tell you and not forget it, okay?" Max nervously twitched his tail but nodded in the affirmative.

"You cannot gain altitude with your wings clipped," The sergeant went on, "so you must head for the neighbor's corn field in your escape. Janice and Francisco, and others that may gather to help in your capture, must watch their footing. Climb a cornstalk and nestle within its top. Even if the searchers are upon you, their eyes will be blinded from the sun when they look straight up from where they are walking in the corn row. If the corn is tasseled, so much the better."

"That is a crazy idea, Sarge, I don't have to escape into any corn row, and eventually they will cut the corn stalks down anyway!"

110

Freedom in Corn Tassels

The sergeant hoped he did not overstep any boundaries. He knew he had gone a little overboard with the cornstalk scheme, but heck, it was only right for a sergeant of his stature to be able to imbibe a little tequila on his day off. Max would understand that.

"That corn is only waist high now, Max. They won't cut those stalks until way after the corn yield, when the stalks are completely dry. We will be in touch again before that happens, one way or the other." Max blinked in disbelief at the sergeant's crazy idea, but his desire to be a detective overrode his good sense.

"You will never have another friend like me, Max. I am just saying that if you ever do try to redeem your freedom, I will know where to find you. Think of it as an insurance policy. I have never worked with a bird before, but I must say I trust your integrity in not betraying a trust like we have established here today, more so than I would of any human. Do you trust me?"

"Yes," Max lied.

"Good! When I open that detective agency let's call it *'Senor García and Max Bird Investigators.'* I see no reason why we can't gather information about those bird marketers to share with the police, do you? After all, a bird is born to fly free."

The sergeant took Max's extended wing in hand as he was leaving. "I'm glad we had this visit today. I may not see you again for some time. You see, my wife is dying, Max. She needs me to help her through this sad period. I am sure you understand."

Max, as a compassionate bird, did understand. He also understood that he was going to keep the inside information about becoming partners in a detective agency tucked securely under his feathers. The thought of it gave him a

111

buzz, but how can a bird that has just been presented with so much sadness and death be thinking of freedom? Whew! Max was sure relieved when the sergeant left.

Max threw out his wings and gave Francisco a surprise embrace when he came outside to see him. "What was that for?" Francisco laughed. "What did you and the sergeant talk about as you were hanging out?"

"You," Max chirped."

"A drink for you…and a shower for you," Francisco
teased as he swished the hose back and forth,
Max giddy from the sprayed 'waterfall'.

15
Denial Bites Back

Jani hollered down, "One egg or two?"

"Please hold them, Jani, I'm watering the garden," Francisco replied.

"A drink for you... and a shower for you!" Francisco teased as he swished the hose back and forth between the flowers and a giddy Max, spraying a waterfall over the parrot as he fluttered wildly in leaps of joy, water trickling down inside his feathers wetting his bare skin in a tickle. In a response of pure pleasure he started singing.

"Let's fly away, yes, fly away with meee...our wings to touch o'er some romantic sea...."

Max inhaled the smell of flower blossoms, noticed the fineness of the iridescent hummingbirds flitting through the vines. He looked into the tiny pond and saw the goldfish swimming and felt grateful.

When the sun came directly over their walled-in world, obliterating the shadows within, Max's eyes became heavy. It was time for his afternoon nap. He dozed off in a delicious dream of a banquet of suet, pineapples, mangos and almonds appearing at his table. He dreamed of the familiar smell of Jani and Francisco, the mingling of their familiar voices.

"Max sure sleeps a lot," Francisco said.

"It's all part of growing up," Jani said. "One day Max dreams he is flying above the trees, the next he takes a nose dive."

Later, as they finished watching the news, Jani turned off the television, hoping Max would tell them what the sergeant had to say during their 'visit.' Max was sitting on her lap, Francisco beside her.

"What did the sergeant have to say about me?" Francisco asked, looking at Max, sure he would spill the beans.

Max reached over and tenderly put a wing on Francisco's thigh. "He told me all about the ahhh... 'events' your family went through, Maestro. I mean about how you all were thrown out into the street, your mother shooting at other women, how the church janitor kicked her and her babies out at night, how she bought a pistol and shot at women who talked to Teo, about the baby's death, and the funeral...and...."

"That sergeant sure covered a lot of territory!" Jani, who had heard most of it before, said. "I wonder why he told you all of that? Tell me, what else did the sergeant have to say, Max?"

"He said you harbored an illegal turtle."

"I didn't go out looking for a turtle. That turtle came to me!" Jani answered, on the defensive.

"Well...it was not *quite* like that, Jani," Francisco interjected.

Jani changed the subject. "It is time you learned about the serpent, to be aware when he comes to call" Jani warned them. "He isn't often seen as he blends in wherever he slithers, he comes in a multitude of guises, ones you might never suspect. When you see his head remember to watch out for the snap of his tail as it feeds on denial. Never forget that denial bites back!"

116

"The sergeant said that if you deny the truth you will be sorry," Max added enthusiastically.

"He did?" Jani and Francisco exclaimed in unison wondering what would lead the sergeant to say that, thinking they needed to be careful of what might be slithering about. Max's lack of perception, his denial of what the sergeant might try to put over on him, made Jani feel irritated. Instead of venting her frustration on Max, which she knew at this point would get her nowhere, she turned on Francisco.

"You deny who you are!" she told him out of the blue at the sight of the Detroit Tigers baseball cap he had plopped on his head backwards.

"… and what about you?" Francisco replied. "You who limps along in Mexico using Spanish words that few of us can understand? What about your denial? Maybe there is no serpent's tail. Maybe we will not be whipped down if the three of us live peacefully here together and don't look back."

"Maybe, Francisco, but only maybe," Jani replied. "There is still the possibility it could appear while you and I are not looking and whip another 30 years out of your life. You are 44 with the experience of a teenager, and I am vulnerable, as I am now 70, but even so, I am still out to prove myself by making use of an education I received in my 50's. And look at Max. He has almost no line of defense, with claws missing on one of his feet. We are certainly a mismatch with society but not with each other, Francisco. We must remain aware of what can happen if we do not protect each other, and we must watch out for Max. He is innocent and did not ask to become part of our world."

Max had been listening, but for once he had nothing to say.

117

Francisco, trying to make sense of what Jani just said, asked, "Did you get into that wine in the refrigerator?" He was concerned for Jani and for Max, who was witnessing her bitterness for the first time.

Jani put her hands on her hips, stretching out her body like a cock rooster in battle mode. Francisco stubbornly stood up to her like a priest in a frock.

"Are you sitting in judgment on me?" Jani said, denying the real reason for her edginess, disparities that she could not put a finger on that made her world shift as if a quake had occurred beneath her, an unsettling feeling, not unlike the time her car had spun on black ice across the freeway and up onto an embankment as the other cars coming toward her went on their way.

Maybe it wasn't *her* children's cries for help that had wakened her at night for the last fifty years, Jani thought. Maybe those cries came from other children, ones that she had erased from her memory that many years ago.

"What's wrong Jani? What made you stagger?" Francisco asked.

"It's hard to explain, Francisco. It's like a change is going to take place in my reality and I don't know what it is."

"And what is your reality?"

"Babies crying," Jani replied. "But you know about that! You have witnessed my handicaps."

"Gee, I haven't. What have *I* missed?" Max said. "I have never seen your handicaps Jefita...other than your loss of hearing and your lack of memory, and your constant need for sleep, I mean.... But those seem like small things compared to *my* limitations. I don't have hands and I don't walk, I waddle... and I am afraid someone will step on me. Often I am treated like I am second class." Max paused, "and when I

118

eliminate at an inappropriate time I could almost *die* of humiliation."

"Handicaps come in different flavors, Max. Their control in inhibiting our lives diminishes as we adjust to them, which we must, because as we get older they multiply. Be thankful for the handicaps you *don't* have."

"Like what, Jefita? It seems like I have them all."

"Hmm, let's see...Suppose you had babies and their feathers were being torn out.... and you watched. But you were in a cage and couldn't save them, and after that they could never fly completely. You felt it was your fault, but was it really? You had no wings then, and when those babies became adults your wings grew back, and one day miraculously your cage door opened and you flew away and tried not to look back, but the sound of babies crying out at night stayed with you."

"But that is just a story, Jani. I think what you're telling us about are *nightmares*!" Max exclaimed.

Jani had once told Max about facing up to *his* disabilities. She thought that she had faced the hard realities she had accumulated through her long life, that denial no longer held her energies captive, that the blank spots that had been scattered through her mind had all been filled in, but why would her children be crying now, when they never cried, she never cried. They were not sissies, and their situation at that time was beyond tears.

The rendition about babies crying that she just told Max and told herself, no longer rang true. Was her memory just the remembering of a remembering, a story repeated so many times it took on a life of its own, its familiarity feeding on itself? She looked at herself in the mirror that night and her children's faces were no longer were there. New images

119

were taking form on the other side of the mirror. Her ears picked up the sound of them, they went 'whew-whooh, whew-whooh.'

It was the sound of an iron lung. Its bellows repeated with a suck and whoosh, the rhythm its mechanical death defying beat. She had heard that sound the other day as Francisco was watching a documentary. She had come running but as she reached the television the polio segment of the program was almost over, it was just a blink of the eye in the historical events of the United States in the 1950s, but Jani got a glimpse of the row of metal caskets on the screen during the polio epidemic. Jani covered her mouth as if she had not seen that incredible site before, sank to her knees, and cried about it for the very first time.

Jani's own ordeal was such a small thing compared to the other children, maybe fifty, maybe a hundred, maybe more in number, whose beds were all scrunched together, the iron lungs lined up against the long wall of the University of Michigan's gymnasium where they were quarantined. The nurses and doctors whispered at night about which child should be left in the iron lungs and which should be taken out to make room for another that had maybe a bigger chance to survive.

Jani could hear the iron lungs in their beat against death. At night beneath dimmed lights she would hear one stop, hear adult feet shuffling about as doctors and nurses whispered about new arrivals. White sheets on metal stands surrounded her bed, the only bed in the gymnasium with them. Jani just had her first period and her mother loudly demanded Jani be moved into the adult ward. The doctors refused. In an effort to silence her mother's daily intrusions the staff rigged up a contraption of white sheets strung across metal bars that had to be clumsily unfolded then refolded each time a nurse came in or left. Nurses often tripped on the stand of Jani's makeshift screen, almost knocking it over as they scurried around in exhaustion taking care of the needs of suffering children as if they were in a never ending game of musical chairs.

The sounds of crying children echoed up the gymnasium walls. Jani caught spatters of conversation from parents who lived far away in the northern part of the state, and the Upper Peninsula, saying goodbye to their children, knowing it might be forever. She reached out with one of the magazines piled on her bed trying to part the curtain with it, wanting to put a face on the tragedies she felt a part of, but was unsuccessful as her feet were strapped to a board at the foot of her bed. Her neck was stiff and flat on her pillow. She spent her days staring at the wall of sheets out of the corners of her eyes as if she could look through them.

Jani's mother never noticed there was another child in that gymnasium. The nurses' hatred of Jani's mother was their main topic of conversation, and they hated Jani *and* her, period, even though they were hidden behind a curtain. She developed a dread of having to ring the bell for a bedpan. She wished she could put it off forever, and one time she held on too long and wet the bed. The nurses that cleaned it up had such contempt for Jani that they turned their faces away from her in disgust when they changed her sheets.

Max was perched beside Jani, studying her face deep in thought, not knowing that a new awareness within her was taking place, but aware that she needed a privacy of space. He was silent waiting for her to be the first to speak. She looked up at him. "Perhaps you are right, Maximo, maybe

121

the cries are nightmares, maybe if I put them in context with the *right* story they will stop!"

Francisco was standing nearby. "What is the right story, Jani? Is it worse than the one of your children crying?"

"No, not worse, just different. I guess I didn't want to bring to mind more sadness, wanted to deny it, but sadness doesn't just go away, it needs to be dismantled and put into a separate box that can be opened when you have the heart for it."

"And when is that, Jani? When is that?" Max inquired with a twist of his beak.

"When loved ones like you and Francisco are near," Jani smiled.

"It wasn't that I wanted a wild turtle to enhance
our pond," Jani explained, realizing she
had done a crime against nature.

16
The Blame Game

"Nobody sees us, they just speed on by," Max screeched, a broken feather flying. "We are in a passing zone; for us it is a no zone, but you don't care, Francisco. *I* am the one responsible for selling your tapestries; all *you* need to do is weave them. How can I do that if nobody sees us! We need neon lights, why hasn't Jani put up neon lights? Flashing lights and balloons that flap in the air with fans blowing under them, and flags, do you hear me, flags, lots of them strung over this lateral with a dead end into a ditch. I want to sell, do you hear me, sell!" Max said, worked up into such desperation that another feather flew out.

"I'm going in to see what Jani is doing and leave you out here to stew by yourself," Francisco said as he walked away. Max hated that word *stew*.

"Max is having another attack of ambition, Jani, and he blames us for everything that doesn't go his way."

"Ambition is part of who Max is, we have to accept that. The blaming is, however…well, not good. What separates the terns from the egrets is their ability to look within for solutions to their problems. Max needs to stop playing the blame game. Maybe we have made it too easy for him not to take responsibility for himself."

"And he keeps bugging me to take him back out on the highway on my bicycle! Taking him out like that was not smart of me. I don't know what I was thinking. I mean I wasn't thinking."

"We need to bring the fact that that can't happen again out into the open, we need to talk with Max about it!" Jani said, "Maybe tomorrow."

"Let's wait until he is in a better mood, Jani. We need to figure out what you need to say."

"Why is this *my* problem, Francisco? You are the one that made it!"

"Isn't it time for Max's wings to be clipped?" Francisco replied, changing the subject.

"Past time, Francisco. Suppose we do not clip them; let his flight feathers grow out."

"I don't think that's a good idea, Jani. It would be too dangerous."

"I know how dangerous it would be, Francisco, but if we keep clipping his feathers it could keep him a teenager forever. He would begin to hate us and we him. If we let them grow out Max would have to learn how to control his emotions, to watch out for his own survival. With our help I believe he is capable of doing that! It would be a fragile time with some setbacks, I might add. Why don't we take today off, sit out front, see what's going on in the neighborhood, think about what we are going to tell Max the next time he asks to go out for a spin on your bicycle?"

Jani, Francisco and Max went to sit outside after seeing a real estate salesman unfold an open sign. They hoped they did not look *too* conspicuous with their three plastic chairs lined up on the street at an angle that would give them the opportunity to observe those that entered and left the vacant house next door.

"That last woman that went in, did she look familiar to you?" Jani asked.

"You always say that," Max replied, peeved, as he tossed his head in the opposite direction, its feathers as flat as a whistle.

"Listen," Jani went on, ignoring Max, "When she comes out, let's give her a closer look!"

Max, precariously balanced on the slippery back of his chair, was being hand fed peanuts by Francisco. Jani was stretched out, ankles crossed, leaning back against a pillow, elbows poking into the air, hands clasped behind her neck. While the three of them waited for the woman to leave; they were the picture of *hanging out*, but their minds were busy wondering how to bring up words they had too long held back.

Max was deep in thought. His bad foot clung to the back of his chair with only two talons. His good foot was left free to manipulate the peanuts, discard their shells, extracting the nuts which he savored, flipping them back and forth on his thick square tongue before gulping them down. He manipulated his claws as if they were fingers, using them with more dexterity than that of a real person.

Francisco was in awe of this incredible creature that had come into their lives, but he sometimes forgot that Max was not human. He was thankful Jani was curious about who might buy the house next door, as it created a diversion. He hoped they did not have to tell Max the extent to which they had to limit his life, at least not on this day.

"There she is!" Jani said as the woman exited the house. "I can't see her face, it is in the shadow of the brim of her hat, but there is something very familiar about the elegant way she walks."

The Blame Game

"And the way she waves, did you see her when she waved good bye to that salesman?" Francisco replied.

Max felt inept trying to keep his balance on the back of his slippery chair. He found it increasingly difficult to keep his frustrations bottled up. He was doing his best to keep his emotions at bay, but he could not resist making a comment. "Who cares who moves in next door? It doesn't make any difference; it doesn't change anything for me!"

Meanwhile, the woman with the golf cart had been traveling along the highway. Fringe had replaced the tassels, but the fiberglass cart was easily recognizable, its imbedded sparkles still glistened in the sun. An elegant Doberman, nose pointed into the wind, was at her side. When she saw the three of them sitting out on the service drive she impulsively made a quick left swerving through traffic, then another left, and came buzzing up the street directly toward them and stopped, not turning off the switch to her engine.

"Hola," she shouted to Max enthusiastically. "How have you been? We are going to be in the Mardi Gras parade this year. Be sure to be there! Be sure to look for us!" Then she sped off.

"I wonder what happened to the Pomeranian, the Pomeranian I saved." Max said.

"I think Max wishes he was that Doberman," Francisco commented.

"And why not? Look at that Doberman and then look at me. I am a shrimp, and if that's not bad enough I am molting again!" Max replied.

"A Doberman? A bird masquerading as a Doberman? Haven't we carried this bird thing too far? Oh my God! Max Bird as a Doberman." Jani leaned back in her chair and let the laughter roll until she choked on her mouthful of peanuts. Tears streamed down her cheeks as Francisco pounded on her back to revive her.

Max threw the whole peanut Francisco had just handed him into the road, stomped his foot, lost his balance, and slipping down the chair's back as if it were a slide, landed upside down in its seat. Righting himself he glared at Jani as if she had pushed him. "When are we going out for another spin on your bicycle?" Max asked Francisco, eyes shifting back and forth, as if in accusation, between him and Jani.

How were they going to make Max understand why he could not be free...but then, maybe freedom *was* worth dying for. What were they going to answer? never? ever? Max had brought the subject to a head. Francisco's eyes opened wide, he dreaded the ugly scene he thought was to come. He blamed himself for this crisis. After a pause that went on almost too long, Jani replied, "Would you like to ride along with Francisco when he goes out in the pickup?"

"Really?" Max replied. "But you said I would *never* be able to do that, Jani. You said that the police might stop us, and that since Francisco doesn't have a drivers license they could arrest us. Francisco said I could *never* drive with him because he might have an accident. Remember when we turned the truck around out front with me perched on your shoulder, Francisco, and as you came too close to the stone wall between us and the main highway, I screamed, STOP! And then you hit the gas pedal instead of the brakes? Boy, did you ever blame me. You said that I could never ride with you again!"

Francisco hung his head in shame as Jani looked at him and shook her head. "I would have told you, but I didn't have the money to fix it. I'm sorry Jani. Please forgive me."

"Well, one more mystery solved, and to think I blamed the neighbors for that smashed fender! When something is an accident there is nothing to forgive, but letting me go on thinking it was the neighbors that did it is terrible!"

Francisco stared at Max. One more time his mouth went off before his motor was running.

"A fender is just a fender," Jani assured them and then she went on to address their real problems: "I have a plan that will enable Max to spend more time in the outside world. The plan comes in two parts."

"Tell us the first part, Jani," Max said in a burst of enthusiasm.

"It involves the use of the small cage you sleep in at night. We can put it in the passenger seat and secure it with the seatbelt. When you accompany Francisco on his errands you can sit on top. Your head should be at about the same level as his and you can see everything that is going on, but remember you have no seatbelt so you must keep a tight hold on the cage at all times in case he has to make a sudden stop."

"No problemo, mi Jefita," Max quivered at this stroke of good fortune. Do you need something from the drug store...or the stationary store? Maybe some more copy paper...pens? Ink?"

"Hold on Max. We haven't talked about part two of this plan, Francisco getting his driver's license."

"I would have had my license a year ago but you refused to pay the 'mordida', Jani."

"I will not pay a thousand pesos in bribes just to make things easy for you! You are almost as spoiled as Max!"

"You know I tried, Jani! The problem was with the road test. Remember how I was told to curb park in a spot between a truck and the police officer, who told me to pretend he was a car? You saw I couldn't do that without running him over. The spot he left me was shorter than our pickup."

"So? I know the advertising in English on the doors of our truck leads them to believe we will pay a mordida like the rest of those from north of the border, but a thousand pesos is a lot of money. You are going to have to give it another try. Paying bribes is just plain wrong! The one that pays out money is as much at fault in encouraging corruption as the one that receives it!" Jani said in indignation.

The following day Max woke even cheerier than usual. "Good morning, Jani, morning, morning," he chirped in a melodious lilt. Max was elated when he saw Francisco come down the stairs holding onto their utility bills and other documentation. "Good morning, Francisco, what a beautiful morning to get a driver's license."

Jani recalled spending half a day standing with Francisco in the hot sun holding onto the necessary paperwork, waiting his turn, only to come away empty handed, and that was a couple of years ago when she was stronger. Jani wondered if she was crazy to go through that again.

"Good luck," Max hollered as Jani and Francisco left.

"Let's stop at Doña Lona's and treat ourselves to breakfast." Jani said.

"But we already had breakfast, Francisco objected. We don't want to be at the end of the line this time!"

"Then let's stop in at Chona's immigration service and see how much she would charge to help us get your license," Jani said.

"Sure, I can take care of that for you," Chona said. "Go across the street to the papeleria and make six copies of all

your papers and give them to me. In two days you can pick
up Francisco's license."

"I can't believe you gave her one thousand five hundred
pesos when we could have taken care of it at the license
bureau for a thousand pesos!" Francisco said.

"Well...It's done, over with, finished, and it's not me that
paid that mordida, it's Chona. My hands are clean." Jani lied
as if she were a mobster who had pulled off a heist.

Jani stood on a flagstone facing the pond looking into the
water thinking about how often she had wronged a right,
how easily she had justified it.   She thought about Maria,
about the 'M' she told Francisco to paint on her shell in red
fingernail polish. She guessed she felt worse about doing
that than any of the other injustices she had done to that
turtle. She could picture Maria struggling to survive on the
lake shore without being noticed by predators, of the red M
giving her position away. Jani felt horrible every time she
thought about it. Her excuses, she knew, were shabby.

"You see," Jani told Max and Francisco, "It wasn't that I
wanted a turtle to enhance the pond, I wanted to help those
kids selling it to raise the money for the hair dryer and stuff
they need to open up a beauty parlor. (I could have just given
them the money, Jani thought.) When Maria kept trying to
get out the door I thought she was looking for a mate, so
when we went to get fish food and I saw her perfect mate
looking up at me from a plastic dishpan on the floor, I did
the only natural thing and bought it. How did I know Maria
would hate the other turtle? That she would mercilessly
attack it, maybe killing it. I thought she would be delighted
to have company, and when we didn't see the other turtle
anymore, I figured it had gone into hibernation early, and
when it never returned I felt...well, sleazy.

132

The Blame Game

Max and Francisco glanced at each from the corners of their eyes. They had not realized Jani felt bad about the second turtle. They should have confessed to giving it a 'free ride' down to the lake.

"You did the wrong thing in buying those illegal turtles, Jani, but don't forget I'm the one that wrote on Maria's back. I can take responsibility for that!" Francisco said."

But the M was not the only reason Jani did not let Maria go free. She looked forward to tossing Maria turtle food when she got up in the morning, of seeing how quick she was when she reached out with her long neck and grabbed it, how her thick tail acted as a rudder, how Elliot got high from playing games with her, dipping his paw in the pond then pulling it out, always a hair out of reach of the snapping turtle's grasp. Jani had to be careful where she stepped when tending the garden lest she lose a strap from her huaraches…or maybe a toe. Maria was a creature needed at Aztec Studios to keep life from becoming too safe, too predictable, too sticky sweet.

One morning Maria wasn't to be found. That wasn't unusual. Then when another day went by, Jani became concerned. "Have you seen Maria?" she asked Francisco.

"A couple of days ago I saw her at the front door," Francisco said. "When I went to the store I may have left the door open and she could have left."

"My God!" Jani said in alarm. "She might have gotten run over by a car."

"I don't think so, Jefita," Max squawked.

"And why not? Jani replied.

"Somebody probably saw her when they were coming home from the store and carried her down to the lake. Isn't that right, Maestro?"

133

The Blame Game

"Thank you for being my conscience, Francisco. Thank you both for doing what was right," Jani sighed in relief but tried to take some of the blame off her shoulders when she said, "I am concerned about the red you painted on her being visible to predators, though. That is the reason I did not take her down to the lake myself, and we certainly could not remove it with fingernail polish remover as she would carry that smell forever!"

Francisco was aware Jani was trying to shift blame onto him and he accepted it because the burden was getting too heavy for Jani to carry alone. Francisco appreciated that when Jani's guilt was exposed, her first reaction was to hide behind an excuse. It was not like her to point a finger in blame. He knew Jani had done an injustice to nature but he loved her in spite of it.

The crocodile eats – "Why don't we ever weave doves and angels?" Max asked Jani.

17
Ponderings of the Soul

Jani set Max on his chair in the great room, plopped down on the sofa, and swung her legs around to hang over one side. Max sat on the chair's back searching for fleas that did not exist. Jani had always been so predictably unpredictable, so easy to divert, so... well...simple. Max studied a woven serpent staring at him from the far wall.

The bells hanging over the open stairway jangled as Francisco came up the stairs, a signal to Jani that someone was approaching. "Max! You have the strangest look on your face," Francisco commented. "Why are you staring at that serpent tapestry in such a strange way?" Max took one last dig at an imaginary flea and flew up onto Francisco's shoulder.

"Why do we weave so many serpents and crocodiles, cougars, and warriors and other scary things? Why don't we ever weave doves and angels?" Max asked Jani.

"Because we are the doves and angels," Jani replied.

"I used to weave LOTS of doves, but Jani said it wasn't healthy," Francisco added with a wry smile. "So now we weave eagles... and egrets and all kinds of *interesting* creatures from Mexico's ancient past."

Ponderings of the Soul

"I think the world we live in is interesting enough, Jani," Max chattered. "Sometimes the human world is *too* interesting. I think we should weave flowers and palm trees...and Jacarandas...yes, shaped like huge open umbrellas...with their purple blossoms hanging off the end...and parrots...yes, lots of parrots living under it, singing songs of love and building nests all over the place...and...."

"And hearts," Francisco added, "with the faces of Elliot and Isabella inside of them, to hang at the end of my loom."

"Maybe I should step out of the room," Jani replied with a straight face, "so the two of you can decide how to run things around here... and while you are at it, you can figure out how you are going to pay for the next shipment of material and pay for the groceries and utilities as well!"

"No, Jani. Please stay," Francisco said. "I'm happy weaving whatever you want. All of our tapestries are beautiful to me, but maybe it is a good idea to understand why you find our prehispanic culture so...fascinating.

"Thank you, Francisco. I need to take a break right now, but you are right, we do need to talk about the tapestries, but a little bit later, okay?"

When Jani left, Francisco got tough with Max. "You are making qualifications about your acceptance of Jani. You need to decide if you are in or you're out. Loving a person in part is no love at all...now let's go downstairs. I need to work on the loom."

Francisco tossed the looms shuttle back and forth, making its faint Tibetan-like tinkle as he had a heart to heart talk with Max, who sat up high on the loom's overhead beam, looking down on the tapestry being woven below. "Humans have many different facets," Francisco explained.

"What are facets, Maestro?"

Ponderings of the Soul

"*Hmm,* let's see, Max. I will give you an example. Think of a person as if he or she were a jewel...in Jani's case a fine one, maybe a diamond. The stone itself would be her soul. The value placed on the stone would depend on its purity. It is likely that stone will later have facets cut into it. These will be polished to create the prisms that make it sparkle in the light, the more finely cut, the more valuable the jewel becomes."

"I bet Jani has *lots* of cuts, Francisco."

"The reason a jewel sparkles is because each prism reflects light from a different source. A person can only be responsible for being the caretaker of their soul. They do not have control over what is cut into their stone, and it is debatable whether the soul has control over what shimmers from its many colors as each prism reflects light from a different source. The prisms form a collective brilliance...as a matter of fact, the stone itself never sees what it reflects, as that light is never turned inward. A person's inner soul is something that must be sensed. If the soul is bad, no matter how brilliantly it sparkles, a wise person will know it. A good soul has a value beyond estimate."

"That sure gives a bird like me a lot to think about, Francisco. I *do* know Jani has a good soul, I just know it!" Max replied, "but aren't those serpents we have hanging on our walls part of what her stone reflects? If we got rid of them, maybe Jani's soul would be happier."

"Why, yes, Max, I suppose it would change the reflection given off from one of her prisms...to one that could be more pleasing. I hadn't thought of that! But on the other hand don't you think our interference might make her soul constricted?"

"Look, Maestro, are you trying to confuse me? Every time I get one of your ideas straight, you mess it up again!"

"No, I'm not trying to confuse you, Max, but still, you must be more patient with Jani. Think of how good she has been to your soul."

"Gee, Maestro. I *do* have a soul, don't I ? Do all birds have a soul, or just me? How about Elliot and Isabella? Do they have souls, do all living creatures have souls, or just the ones that belong to our family?"

"What do you think, Max?"

"I think a heart that beats must have a soul, but where is it located? Since I'm small does that mean my soul is less valuable than your soul, that a big person's soul is better than a small person's soul?"

"Whoa, Max. Those are difficult questions. Souls don't have a size; they can be found...or not found, in any creature. Souls transcend all earthly things, the aura of their spirits can't be held in the palm of a hand because there is nothing of matter to hold, so their size can't be measured by a ruler or weighed like a cup of flour. It can't be denied, however, that a soul lies inside of me and you and most living creatures. Maybe we create them, maybe they are a gift from the heavens, we don't know. We are just humans...or birds...we can't know everything!"

"Sounds like an interesting discussion," Jani said as she entered the room.

"It's interesting all right!" Max replied. "First Francisco told me the soul was a stone and then he told me it was a spirit. Which am I to believe? Do they cancel each other out?"

"I was *trying* to explain a concept to Max in a way a bird-brain could understand!" Francisco snapped, fed up with answering Max's questions then having his answers critiqued.

140

"Hey, what's this with the name calling?" Jani said. "This is not a cantina. Look, Max, Francisco is just trying to help you. What he does is use metaphors. He uses a thing to represent a concept so you can picture it in your mind. It is a very good way to explain the unexplainable. A metaphor is also a handy figure of speech to use when what you feel and what you think are not in agreement."

"Got it, Jani," Max lied. "Feathers!" he thought. "Jani is even more confusing than the Maestro."

"Good," Jani replied. "I love metaphors! That's what I find so fascinating about the ancient indigenous peoples. They lived their life in metaphor; their pictographs were in metaphor, their gods, even themselves. They believed they were vessels that carried spirits which would live on forever after they died, that their bodies would be magically reincarnated into different combinations of animals, like they could return to be part deer, revered for its intelligent sensibilities, part rabbit for its ability to procreate, or cougar for its elegant fierceness, and possibly part bee so they could pollinate the beautiful gardens at Chapultepec Park. The peoples of that time thought they could return to this earth as all of those creatures, imagine that! You can see why the Aztecs offered to sacrifice themselves on those altars, offered to have the priests tear their hearts out to appease the gods so that others, like those that screamed below the temple, could have another day of the sun. What a better, more honorable end could a spirit's vessel have?"

Francisco intervened. "Let me help explain metaphors." "Look," he said addressing Max, "Jani was using an *old fashioned* metaphor when she used the word vessel to refer to a human. Another way of putting it would be to say that a person was a suitcase that was filled with spirits. Do you understand now?"

141

"I think I do," Max now truthfully replied, "but what I really want to know about are the serpents, the serpents we have hanging on our walls!"

"What we have on our walls are *plumed* serpents," Jani replied. "They are actually part bird, and now that you have learned about metaphors you will be able to understand them. In Mexico there have been droughts where the land has dried up, where almost nothing was left living. The few humans that survived believed the world was coming to an end. One day, serpents emerged through cracks in the earth at the scent of moisture in the air and the rains came. They became a symbol of hope and survival. How natural that they combined with birds that flew to insure that messages were received by the gods that resided in the heavens, messages asking them for the gift of sun or rain."

"You mean our serpents are good? But I thought all snakes were bad, Jani, that's what I thought!"

"We are often afraid of things we do not understand, my bird," Jani replied.

"Then make us understand how the Aztec priests could line innocent people up and tear out their hearts, Jani, and most of them were captives that didn't want to die. How could thousands watch? They were blood thirsty people, Jani. How could you believe any of it was interesting?" Francisco asked.

"The Aztecs, all of our ancient peoples for that matter, are a history lesson on the human condition, Francisco. We can study them and recognize who we are. I like the idea of my spirit living on through other life, but I do not like the idea of man killing man, or animal, for that matter."

"Or bird, Jan, or bird," Max squawked, although over time he had become conditioned to Jani and Francisco being carnivores.

"I have eaten so many Porky the pigs, Elsie the cows and other living creatures, Jani said...but I try to keep this carnage out of my reality. When I catch myself watching live coverage of innocent victims of war being killed, cultures being wiped out, nature being destroyed, while I sit there and watch it on television, I wish I belonged to another species. I have to view it as though I were a fox or a jaguar, for can you blame a carnivore for being a carnivore? The only difference between us and the Aztec is we do not look into the faces of victims and scream."

"How terrible, how awful, even some of my own species are killers, but there *is* a solution, there is!" Max said, as he jumped up and down all a-twitter, wing tip pointed into the air. "We don't have to think about bad things, we don't have to know what the world is doing outside of our cage. We can sell that television! I don't watch it anyway."

"You don't have to make excuses for being human, Jani. You have a good soul," Francisco added.

18

Green Cards, Vendors
& Polio

Francisco remembered his father proudly tending his rose garden when he lived in Bakersfield. It was beside the leaning shack he lived in when he was a pruner in a vineyard that sprawled across California's coastal sky. He lived apart from the other workers and their families who lived in a community of trailers near a small city nearby. He was monitored by the health department, a practical solution for the agricultural workers suffering from tuberculosis who needed to keep working lest their families in Mexico go without food.

"I slept on a mat on the floor beside Teo's bed when he worked in the vineyards in California, Max. I rolled it up first thing in the morning in case a social worker came by to check on him and caught me." Francisco said.

"Caught you for doing what, Maestro?"

"For being an illegal," Francisco replied. "Teo would step over me on his trips to the bathroom to cough up blood before he went to work. He felt terrible about not being able to keep up with my brothers who worked the field beside him. They were a team and had to make up for his slowness, and they could no longer make bonus to take their girlfriends out on Saturday nights."

"But you told us you had a green card!"

"I did. My first job was working as a woodcutter. Then the boss gave me the job of driving the big semis loaded with lumber down the mountain, as I was more serious than the others. When I turned eighteen he got me the green card and we went into town together to apply for my driver's license, but I couldn't pass the eye exam. He took me to get glasses but they found I was blind in one eye."

"I'll bet the bosses didn't let you drive those big trucks down from the mountain anymore! Gosh, that's too bad, Maestro, that is *really* too bad!" Max remarked.

"But they did, Max, and on the following Saturday, on my last trip down the mountain, after a payday drunk, one of our logging crews blocked the road ahead waving their arms for me to stop. I slowed down and they jumped on the piles of lumber in back with their bundles of dirty laundry and would not get off, insisting they ride with me into town to the laundromat. Foolishly I let them. When the boss found out that was the end of my job and my green card."

"Gee, I'm sorry they fired you, Maestro. What did you do then?"

"I was the only one with a green card and I lost it! I was too ashamed to call my mother in Mexico to tell her my regular money would not be coming in. I knew my father had smuggled two of my younger brothers across the border and were near Bakersfield working the fields in an effort to keep my ten younger brothers and sisters left in Mexico in school, so that's where I headed with the money from my last paycheck. As I approached the vineyard the first time, I turned back, too ashamed to face them. So I drifted, eating

146

Green Cards, Vendors & Polio

little, picking up odd jobs and sleeping on the streets. I
remember growing mushrooms with an old Chinese man,
and picking kiwis, and remember a real pretty white girl that
smiled at me, but most of that time I don't remember at all.
Anyway, eventually I found my way to Bakersfield to sleep
on the mat beside Teo, as I said."

When Francisco stayed with his father he had circled the
vineyards, running around and around its perimeter. When
he stopped, voices overtook him. The voices were of his
mother, sisters, aunts and nieces, crying out, *"help me.
Francisco, please help."* He ran by the fields where his
father and brothers were pruning grapevines, fingers and
scissors flying, a specialty perfect for men who were once
proud weavers from Jalisco. He didn't stop or slow down,
sometimes he even speeded up, and sometimes he didn't
know who they were. Other voices shouted. *"Run,
Francisco, run, where's your green card. They will throw
you in jail; you will rot in prison, run, run! "* And he did.
One day he spun off the vineyard's perimeter and kept
going. Teo searched and searched for him but he had
vanished. The family had given him up for dead. It was
years later that he turned up back in Mexico.

"I was shocked my family had given me up for dead.
Where did the years go? They say one morning they looked
out and saw me standing in the street before their front gate.
'Where were you?' I remember them asking me. *'Where am
I?'* I replied. I want to find my way home."
"That's what I thought, the very same thing, Maestro!
When I was put up for sale by the bird vender in Jocotepec, I
kept asking myself, *'where am I, I want to go home!'* Gee,
we are not different; we are the same, we are exactly

147

alike...well, almost!" Max fluttered, excited at the very idea of it. "...anyway, we *would* be, Maestro, if *you* grew feathers!"

"For years I had tried to find my way home," Francisco continued, "and when I got there I discovered home no longer existed. My family had moved from the small village of Ajijic to the city of Puerto Vallarta. There, living in three rooms, I found my mother, sick and blind, being nursed by sisters who had grown into women I hardly recognized.

"My mother and my younger brothers and sisters felt they had been abandoned by my father and brothers living in Bakersfield as less and less money came in. My mother had visions of Teo living in luxury, dancing at night with other women. My younger brothers were resentful that my brothers in California married, had gone on to have children of their own, and were fuming at the report of one of them buying a king size mattress while *they* slept on the floor. I tried to defend my brothers in California, whose wives also worked in the fields, and my father who was sick. I thought, *'this can't be, this just can't be!'* They gave me a place to stay on the roof. "

"...and I thought that too, Maestro." Max added. "I thought *'this can't be'* after the vendor bought me at auction from the thieves market, telling me he was taking me home to his family and then sticking me up on top of a wobbling stack of cages to be sold on the streets of Jocotepec."

"I'm sorry, Max," Francisco sighed. This must be the day of bad stories!"

"What bad stories?" Jani asked as she walked into the studio, munching on an apple.

148

"Ours, I mean the stories of Max... and myself." Francisco told her.

"Gee," Max squawked, "you are so old, I bet you are packed with *lots* of stories, at *least* five times more than me!"

"Maybe," Jani laughed, "but let's hear more of yours! Tell us about that vendor that bought you."

"You saw him. He is the one that sold me to you! He was down on his luck, way down on his luck, he looked pretty sad didn't he?" Max said, once again trying to flesh out a story from the remnants of vague thoughts he had retained from the time he was a baby bird, memories he occasionally brought back to mind, then built on to make them part of his reality. This was one human trait that he was very good at.

"Yes, I remember him," Jani replied. "He looked pretty decrepit, leaning up against all of those cages secured with strings, wires, spit and whatever, bars patched with tin can tops and hunks of wire screening. His weary eyes peered into my purse in a way that made me feel quite uncomfortable."

"He was not a bad man. He loved his grandchildren and maybe he loved me too...but in a *very* strange way."

"...Like how?" Francisco asked.

"He began to brag about me, Max Bird, but at that time I was nothing, just a bleary eyed infant. It was after we entered the cantina, after he gulped down a couple of tequilas. He told the owner of the cantina that I was a special bird with the heart of an eagle, said the evidence was in my missing claws, that I had hung onto a tree branch so fiercely when they tried to rob me from my mother's nest my claws snapped off!"

"Oh my God!" Jani said, "My poor little bird!"

149

Green Cards, Vendors & Polio

Max hated it when Jani talked to him like that but he continued. "...A customer with a wide brimmed sombrero hollered out to the vendor, 'You sold me on *that* parrot! How much do you want for him?' My vendor hollered back, 'He is *my* bird and he is priceless, and he is not for sale!' After that whenever someone tried to buy me he would talk them out of it."

"How is it he wound up selling you to me...and at such a low price?"

"First, I will tell you how much I wanted to be wanted, Jani ...as I remember that very clearly. I didn't know about being wanted until the vendor said he wouldn't sell me. In my innocence I thought that meant I was to belong, belong to this man, to his family, to his home. Whatever it turned out to be, I thought, was better than no home at all...much better. I didn't think about my future, it didn't matter; the only thing that mattered to me was that I was wanted... but that didn't last long."

"Mira, abuelito, you must sell that parrot soon. Your grandchildren need books and school shoes!" the vendor's wife said when we came home. Every day the vendor increased the amount he wanted for me. His wife got more and more angry; finally, shoeless and bookless the grandchildren were told they could no longer go to school. That's when he sold me to you."

"I feel terrible I paid him so little for you, Max, but I emptied my purse, I gave him all the money I had!"

"....And the vendor doesn't seem strange at all, Max." Francisco added. "I bet you even missed him after Jani bought you!"

"I won't miss him stopping to pet my bad foot when he hobbles along on his. I won't miss that eerie feeling,

150

Francisco, *and that's for sure*...and one day when the vendor had a toothache and the straps on his huaraches gave way, he said to me, 'I saw you flirting with that young couple over there!' Then his good sense left him and he began screaming at me like a crazy man for everyone on the block to hear. 'Okay, mister wimp feathers,' he shouted, 'do you think they can give you a better bird cage than I? Why don't you fly on over there and ask them? But you can't fly can you? Your wings are underdeveloped and when you grow up someone will clip them. You will *never* be better off than you are right now here with me!"

"Wow," Jani whistled. So much for being wanted! I see now why you don't miss him.

"Thank you for buying me from the vendor. I'm *so* sorry I bit you when you put your hand into the bag. I never expected to have anything really good happen to me. I expected the worse, you see, as I didn't know any better at that time."

"But, my bird," Jani told Max, "You have a home now. You are safe here with us and you *are* wanted."

"I know, Jani," Max replied. "It's just that sometimes I get the feeling that life here is too good, that something bad must be hiding in a corner."

"The three of us will be together forever, Max. There is nothing bad hiding in a corner." Francisco reassured him as Max buried his beak under Francisco's armpit, embarrassed by his fluttered feathers.

"*Forever is a long time*," Jani stated softly.

"I'll bet Max thinks *your* childhood was just one long vacation. But that wasn't true, was it?" Francisco replied.

"No it wasn't. Maybe nobody's childhood was. Still I hear others tell stories about happy childhood memories and think

151

I must be an ungrateful daughter for remembering so many bad ones. Even though my mother did not want me, she loved me, and would have forgiven the harsh judgment I paint her with when I write, as her whole life was one that had the necessity of a tough forgiveness.

"I remember the ill-fated vacation I went on with my parents when I was twelve and that cabin on that lonely treeless stretch of blacktop that separated it from Lake Michigan. My father had rented it sight unseen and was bringing the groceries in when mother announced that she would not stay in that desolate place. They decided to go to Traverse City to 'look around,' leaving me in the cabin alone because I was 'not feeling well.'"

"*I* would never have left you there alone!" Francisco said, "When you are not feeling well I sleep on the couch downstairs in case you need me!"

"… You *would* think my mother would have noticed that the bag of groceries they left on the counter was undisturbed, that the hot dogs were uneaten, the potato chips not opened. The motherly thing to do would have been to check on me when she and my father returned to the cabin in the middle of the night, but my mother had never been mothered, so she did not understand these things. What she thought she understood was that my getting polio was *her* fault."

"The shore of rocks covered with only a thin layer of sand made wading into Lake Michigan difficult. I had made a mistake leaving my shoes on shore, still, I had never heard of anyone swimming with their shoes on. My plan was to wade in until the water topped my shoulders, then test my new swimming skills by swimming back to shore. I had waded quite a distance and the water was still only waist deep, and I was feeling dizzy so I headed back. My legs buckled up under me, and with my arms flailing I kept throwing myself forward eyeing the shore... the shallower the water the heavier my body. Finally, my legs becoming useless I dropped to my knees and in a half crawl, I continued on, falling over, pushing myself back up, choking on swallowed water. Just when I thought I was not making headway, that I was sure to drown, the shoreline started rising. I crawled out onto shore, scraped and hurting. Not until then did I become aware I was trembling with fever.

"Didn't anybody see you, Jefita? Wasn't there anybody around?" Max asked.

"...I remember eyeing my shoes a few yards away," Jani went on, "but decided against using the energies I had left to go after them. I made it to the road that ran just in front of the cabin. I lay down beside it to rest, hoping someone would come by and help me, then I picked myself up to stagger across the blacktop as it seared the soles of my feet. I made it into the cabin and into bed, still wearing my swimsuit and passed out. I woke to a teeth chattering cold, like I had never felt before. I managed to take the cushions off the chair, the towels, and all of my clothes, and piled them on top of the blankets that covered me. That is how my parents discovered me after they woke up the next morning."

"What did your parents do then, Jani?" Francisco asked.

"It was the year of the big polio epidemic. They bundled me up and laid me in the back seat of the car and found a telephone in the nearest town to call the doctor for instructions. We were four hours from the University of Michigan hospital in Ann Arbor. My father drove like there was no tomorrow. Nobody spoke; the car was dripping with guilt. I *wished* I could *wish* to go home, but I never ever felt

I had one. I wished I felt kinder, more in touch with the damaged people that were my parents, but I could not."

When Jani stopped speaking ,the three of them fell silent. It seemed there was nothing else to say. Only to break the silence Francisco asked Max as he removed him from his perch, "Ready for bed, Max?"

After too much wine, Jani bounded down the stairs,
Francisco clutching onto her collar and shirttail,
Max on his shoulder squawking, "STOP, Jani, STOP!"

19

Dancing to the Moon

Francisco's heart broke at the thought of the sergeant and Jani "being together." He studied English so he could communicate with Jani better, studied to catch up to where he could have been if he had not lost so many years. He could never catch up to Jani, though, as she kept advancing at a rate that almost matched his, and when he got older, she got older. He imagined that Jani would never get old enough to die. She would outlive him. He could picture her wrapped up in her old snowflake robe listening to Max, middle aged and perched on her lap, and although she had become totally deaf, writing the stories he told her, stories of the three of them, of serpents' tails and crocodiles captured in their weavings, and birds of peace, yes, many birds of peace... and angels. He would leave her many drawings of angels.

Jani loved Francisco too much. She knew he desired to have a woman. She fantasized that when she died he would return to California where he would meet a nice American woman at a singles group, a woman who had a good job and some children that Francisco could be father to, a woman that would value him as much as she herself did. She savored the thought of his joyful face as he rejoined the older group of his siblings, the ones that could never return to Mexico, had never seen Francisco's transformation, this man that had been like a second father to them when they were young. She could give him this gift by marrying him. It was the only way he could get back across the border. She planned to do this on her 80th birthday, when she was really in the homestretch of life, if they were still together and happy. But she knew life constantly changed and that the future could not be foretold, that they both needed to stay open for what may be in store for them.

Max saw the look of interest on Francisco's face when the pretty woman came to sell him Avon products he didn't use, how he responded to her smile. He dreamed of her moving in. Her three children would liven up their place, give it new energy. She would do the dishes; take over Francisco's homemaking chores, freeing him to weave all of the time. Jani would like that. Then, the sergeant would move in. He imagined the sergeant and Jani romancing at night. He bet she would like that too. In the daytime he and the sergeant would go off to work in their private patrol car. It would have a picture of him on the side with the caption: *Max Bird and the sergeant will solve all of your crimes.* They would stop in daily at the donut shop, swing up on a stool and, munching on donuts, exchange information with the policemen who stopped in there. The more Max thought about it, the more he realized he needed a plan to make it all happen.

Jani began wondering if she had made Francisco feel too hemmed in, too obligated to her, for why else would he want her to get to know the sergeant 'better.' Besides, maybe it was time she spiffed herself up, bought more feminine clothes, face tightening cream, eye liner to enhance her blue eyes. She knew Mexican men loved blue eyes. The sergeant

158

Dancing to the Moon

was maybe 62, she would not lie to him about being older, but she could tell him she was only 5 years older, which she would not need to consider being a lie, because she *felt* 5 years younger. Her second husband was 20 years younger, a fact hidden from Francisco so he would not get confused about their relationship. Besides, she was confused enough. Sometimes it was apparent that his mind was clearer than hers.

Jani went shopping. She found two dresses that were perfect for enticing the sergeant. One dress was 890 pesos, and the other was 940 pesos. The shoes, open toed and sexy, were 790 pesos. Of course new "undies," and a manicure and hair styling were needed. She was willing to do all of this but when she discovered the skin tightening crème was 490 pesos she balked. She had never needed to buy skin tightening créme before. When she added it all up it came to a whopping 5,500 pesos. Jani realized she could almost afford a vacation for that amount of money.

"Jani," Max chirped more cheerfully than ever. "You would never guess who is downstairs. It is the sergeant. I saw him from the top of my cage walking along the road and whistled. He is here to visit us!"

"I wish you hadn't asked him in, Max," Jani replied.

"I told him we were very sorry to hear about his wife dying," Max went on in a high degree of excitement, eyes flashing as he jitterbugged on the floor twittering between sentences. "I told him that he needed the companionship of a good woman to help him through his grief. Isn't that right, Francisco? That's what he needs. I told him about you, that you had a need for romance. C'mon, Jani, come tell him you are sorry about his wife dying!"

"No," Jani replied. Max's feathers fell flat.

"OH, I understand, Jani. You want him to see you looking less....umm...natural. I'll tell him to come back later...Or maybe tomorrow?"

"Never," Jani replied.

"What have you got against happiness?" Max indignantly spouted.

"The pursuit of happiness is a modern idea, Max. You need to learn that it is not a natural state for humans."

"It is no fun around here anymore! Why can't we have more fun?"

"Fun is not lasting, Max. Once you are done having it, it is over. Satisfaction is where it's at. Satisfaction stays with you."

"Feathers," Max screamed in a temper tantrum. "I am going to tell the sergeant I want to live with him, and the next time you go to cut my wing feathers I am going to bite your fingers because I am going to fly away!" This time Jani did not brush Max's words off lightly.

"Then pack up your feathers and go, smarty....whoops. I am sorry I said that, Max. I didn't really mean it, my mouth just ran off before my mind was in gear..."

Max was shocked. How could she say that? He thought her love was infinite, a mother's love. Could she dump him and not look back, like Teo did? Could she throw him out on the street to be run over by a car? Maybe the sergeant would not want him either and then what would he do? Who would want a bird who had forgotten how to warble? He crawled up on Francisco's shoulder, buried his beak deep into his own breast feathers and wept.

"Max's mood swings have really gotten out of hand. What are we ever going to do with him?" Francisco said. And I don't think *he* even sees what is going on!"

160

"I think I do, "Jani replied as she removed Max from Francisco's shoulder and held him to her, cupping his head in her warm hand as she crooned softly. "It's hormonal. It's not his fault. Can you imagine this little bird would think living with a police sergeant would be more fun than living with a couple of artists? Francisco, please go explain to the sergeant, in a very nice way, that I am not interested. Tell him there is no need for him to come back."

"I would be happy too, Jani," Francisco replied with considerable relief. How could he ever have thought Jani would be interested in romancing a man? She was above and beyond that.

"I told him," Francisco said with satisfaction, happy that Jani did not want the sergeant, happy they did not have to discover whether he was friend or snake. Max's beak peeked out from in-between one of Jani's fingers.

"I could go for a glass of wine, a big glass, and diet cola for you, Francisco, and peanuts for the three of us...and how about some music, happy music, dancing music. We can go up on the top of the lookout and watch the sun go down over the lake while we listen to music, yes? Could that be arranged, mi compañero?" Jani sweetly asked Francisco.

"But you said you didn't like fun, Jani," Max peeped, unable to resist the urge to make a sarcastic comment.

"We are not going up on the lookout to have fun, Max. We are going up to celebrate. Joy and celebration, laughter and tears are as old as mankind."

Max was still cuddled against her breast as she headed up the stairs, Francisco following with the CD player and a bottle of wine.

The angle of the sun cast moody shadows across the barrancas of the Sierra Madre. It cast a warm glow on Max,

161

Dancing to the Moon

Jani and Francisco as they stood on the lookout paying homage to its setting. A fisherman's boat could be seen heading in for the night, on their still volcanic lake, its hand-hewn hull smoothed by the tides of time.

Francisco brought up a plastic chair for Jani and stool for their drinks and peanuts. Max rode on his shoulder. Francisco inserted a CD into the player. Dancing music with a strong bass foot-stomping beat began to play, Mexican country music. Max rapidly beat his wings triple time as Francisco gripped his feet, the arc of his neck stretched to its maximum, every group of feathers a twitter in response. Francisco began to dance, picking up his knees, stomping the floor with the heel of his boot as only a Jalisco man could. Max barely hung on, the precariousness adding to his elation.

Jani had decided that on that night she would not set a good example for her loved ones. She drank her third glass of wine. She forgot the pain that would come tomorrow as she rose from her seat and joined Francisco and Max in dance. She danced as if there was no tomorrow, as if she was still in her youth, as if it had never left her. Francisco swung her on his arm while Max screeched to the heavens, to the stars above, and they went round and around and there was nobody there to stop them. Isabella and Elliot stood hairs apart, at peace with each other at last. Together they sat on the edge of the low wall as if it were a pew, paying respect to the celebration.

Francisco stopped dancing when Jani poured her fourth glass of wine. He realized that they were three stories up into the sky, the wall was low, the stairs were steep. He reached for Jani's arm as if they were to continue dancing, and huddled her down the back metal stairway. In a half stagger she quickly leapt through the great room. Just in

162

time he was able to latch onto her back collar and shirttail as she tripped down the last flight of stairs, Max hollering, "Stop, Jani, stop!"

Catching his breath, Francisco put an exhausted Max into his cage. Jani stood beside him, panting. Max buried his beak into his breast feathers and fell asleep, the aftermath of the highest of a natural high.

"Look at Max. Have you ever seen a bird so sweet?" Jani said, heart pounding. She partially folded the satin cover that made Max feel safe at night yet left enough of his cage uncovered so they could continue to admire him.

Francisco put his warm palm on Jani's shoulder. They stood gazing at Max in pride and wonder, the universal picture of proud parents everywhere. Max opened his left eye a peep to bask in their bliss.

"If I learn to fly maybe I won't know how to land.
Maybe wind currents will sweep me up and take me to
where I don't want to be," Max explained.

20
Somewhere Over the Rainbow

"Who could be at the door this late at night?" Jani said to Francisco, apprehensively choosing to ignore it. Then the doorbell rang again.

Jani and Francisco opened the glassed-in front, unlocking the big metal doors that covered the entrance at night. A woman stood alone, eerily lit by the neon tubes that bathed the front of the gallery at night. An African grey parrot was on her shoulder.

"I saw your lights on and couldn't wait to tell you the good news! I bought the house next door," the woman said.

It was the señora in blue linen, now more softly dressed in pale peach. Diamonds still glittered from her fingers. The parrot acknowledged Jani and Francisco with a twist of her neck, arrogantly flipping her feathers, then snootily turned her head away. "I just know Lu Lu will *love* Max," the señora said.

Jani and Francisco backed up a couple of steps to create a little distance. The señora stepped inside.

Jani's energy, holding on to see her through this wonderful time, suddenly left. Still out of breath, knees wobbling, she leaned against Francisco. He put his arm around her. Jani didn't know how she was going to cope with the señora yet again. Sweat still dripping from Francisco's hair now traveled down the side of his nose.

"Oh my goodness! I hope I didn't interrupt anything!" the señora exclaimed when she realized the state they were in.

"No, no, you didn't interrupt *anything*!" Jani and Francisco replied in unison. They backed up a couple more steps, shamefaced under her scrutiny for having been so joyful that night.

"Are you sure?" The señora looked past them, past the courtyard, wondering if the old loom was still inside Francisco's workroom, wondering if life still went on in their studios as she remembered it.

"How absolutely lovely your place looks lit up at night!" she raved. "Is it at all possible for Lu Lu to meet Max tonight?"

"Maybe tomorrow," Jani reluctantly replied, stepping forward as the señora backed out the door.

"Maybe tomorrow," Francisco repeated as he began to gently close the metal doors without them seeming to be shut in her face. "Thank you for coming. I am sorry Max is sleeping. Yes, we are happy to be your neighbors, yes do come back, do," he stammered as he shut the door completely, much to his and Jani's relief.

"Maybe I could have told her to just go away and not come back, like I told the sergeant," Francisco said after she left. But he wondered. *How could they have behaved differently? They were just being themselves.*

Francisco pecked Jani on the lips, as he always did before she headed off to bed. He walked up the long stairway and through the great room to his bedroom, once the gallery's storeroom, off the back veranda, stepping over a broom and dustpan. He entered and sat on the edge of his bed.

Francisco hoped that nothing would *ever* come between Jani and him...or them and Max. A pencil was nearby. He drew his favorite scene on the wall beside his bed, a little girl, arms held up to the heavens, an arc of doves extending from her hands, his father's traditional pattern. The act of drawing this scene always gave him a feeling of peace. He was commemorating that night as three of them had come together and they had been blessed by the spirits and they had rejoiced in the celebration of it and Jani had leaned on him in an act of trust. He drew angels around his tiny bedroom window thinking of Max, of the look of innocent peace on his face that night before he fell asleep. He signed the drawings of angels at the base of the window and recorded the date; and then he slid down into the soft silken sheets Jani had given him, knowing truly that they had visited heaven.

Max woke Francisco early the next morning singing in his very best form. "Oh, what a beau-tiful morning, oh what a beau-tiful day, I'm full of wing flapping feelings, but I'm not gonna' flyyyay a-way!

"Oh, how we danced...to the moon, to the stars, to the heavens, that looked down upon us and blessed our family," Max thought. "Oh, how good it felt to be part of Jani and Francisco, as he held onto my legs so securely I could flap-flap with all of my might and pretend I was soaring, my head facing into the wind, braving it, then dashing back and forth in a dance before landing back onto our rooftop into the arms of those that love me. Oh, what a life, what a glorious, beautiful life." Max sighed as he lay on his back on the kitchen table , short bird legs suspended, feet splayed out

167

flat, talons curled under, Francisco's big hand covering his belly, his index finger scratching under Max's right wing. "I don't ever want to be alone again, Maestro. I want to spend the rest my life with you and Jani."

"I haven't seen you test your wings without me holding you. Your flight feathers must have grown out by now," Francisco replied.

"I'm afraid to, Maestro. When I flap my wings hard and begin to lift, caution stops me. If I start flying maybe I won't know how to stop, maybe wind currents will sweep me up to where I don't want to go. I wonder how far I would fly before my strength gave out, whose cornfield I would land in, maybe one far away where no one would think to look for me."

"I could tie a string to your ankle, Max, like you are a kite, and if you go too far, I can reel you back in," Francisco and Max both laughed.

"What are you guys laughing about?" Jani said, entering the kitchen.

"Freedom," Francisco replied. "What are you going to do with *your* freedom when you have killed the demons that have kept you from it, Jani? What would you like to be free to do?" Francisco asked, only a little worried about her reply.

"Why, live here with you," Jani said, not having to think about it. "And you?"

Francisco had to give it some thought. Finally he replied, "Go to the plaza for ice cream, a dairy whip, chocolate, with nuts on top…with you…and I'd like to take Max with us this time."

"Is that ALL you want to be free to do?" Jani asked. Francisco's contented face gave her the answer.

"But there is too much activity on the plaza to have Max ride on your shoulder, Francisco, besides, who knows what some flight of fancy would lead him to do in all of that excitement!"

"I can't hold onto him and hold onto you at the same time, Jani. What are we going to do?" They looked at Max. Max looked at them, scratching behind his ear, *knowing* they would come up with an answer.

"I could tie a few feet of yarn around his ankle and attach it to my watch band...like a leash...like insurance, or I should say assurance, that his instincts would not make him do anything foolish," Francisco said.

Max's feathers peevishly flattened at the coarseness of this solution, *still* he could not think of a better one. What color of yarn should he ask for... blue, yellow, multicolored? Yes, multicolored, he thought... and the deed was done, and they were off for ice cream on the Plaza.

Francisco, Max, and Jani stood behind a man in a tall sombrero as they waited to order. "I'll eat the nuts off of Francisco's cone," Max said, clutching onto Francisco's shirt sleeve. "No need to order one for me!" The man in front of them turned around. It was Sergeant García. He stared at the yarn tied to Max's ankle, his eyes traveling down to the other end tied to Francisco's watch band.

"What's this?" he asked, pointing to the yarn in disdain. "It's just like I told you, isn't it, Max?" the sergeant said.

"Told him what, told him what?" Jani demanded, sparring for a confrontation.

The sergeant turned around and paid for his ice cream then faced them again as he turned to leave. "Remember what I told you, Max. You do not want to be tied up like some old mare waiting to be fed, do you?" He said with a nod toward Jani as Francisco handed her a cone.

"You can keep your cornfield idea, Mister Sergeant," Max said. "You've been trying to turn me against my own family! I see *now* what you've been up to!"

"Stupid bird," the sergeant answered, "Letting yourself be tied up like a dumb girl! Our private arrangement is off!" Jani had had enough of the sergeant. She smashed her ice cream right into his face.

With one chomp of his hooked beak, Max severed the length of yarn that Jani and Francisco thought was holding him. Max made a couple of aggressive swoops around the sergeant's head. The sergeant made a quick retreat, the palm of his hand holding his sombrero to his head as he fled.

Max didn't stop flying, he swooped yet wider and wider as Francisco and Jani screamed, "**NO**, Max, **NO!**" Max looked down at their anguished faces but could not stop. He made several passes around the plaza before making a soft landing in exhaustion, on the hot dog vendor's umbrella, his out of shape wings no longer able to flap. Francisco rescued their embarrassed bird, apologizing to the hot dog vendor whose customers had scattered. Hanging his head in shame, Max said, "I'm so sorry I flew away like that, my wings got out of control!"

Jani, trembling from the fear they might lose Max, tied the rebozo that hung around her shoulders into a knot at her side. With both hands she carefully placed Max inside of its folds as if he was as fragile as a raw egg. The rebozo swayed back and forth as Jani walked, like the hammock on their rooftop when Francisco pushed him, secret times, times when there were just the two of them, and now it was just he and Jani snuggled together, hearts beating as one, and Max felt the wholeness of it, of their life together.

170

Somewhere Over the Rainbow

Francisco was vigilant as he held onto Jani. "What would she do without him?" he thought. "How many times had he kept her from falling on these stone streets? How many sets of glasses had he saved, how many broken bones? What would he do without her? Without her, there had been no life. What would they do without Max? It was Max that made them a family."

Max felt secure tucked inside Jani's rebozo as they walked along toward their pickup and home. "Why didn't I think of carrying Max around in my rebozo before? That sure was a dumb idea, taking a bird out on a leash. Why did we do that?" Jani asked Francisco.

"Because Max wanted to be free, remember? But free to do what? We are not free and we *like* it that way!" Francisco said.

"But I am writing a book about us wanting to be free!" Jani exclaimed.

"We are not free and we don't want to be." Francisco stated emphatically.

"When we get home can I get clipped?" Max asked. "This has been too much freedom for me!"

The next morning, bursting through a halo the color of sweet mangos, a sun of the most golden yellow made its home nestled in a velvet sky, the purest of pristine blue. Max could be heard belting out a hopeful, yearning song whose notes floated out of the house and vibrated through the courtyard.

"Some-where over the rainbow, way up high, there's a land that I dreamed of... once in a lulla-bye. La la, La la la la la, La la lahhh....

Afterword

Life goes on at Aztec Studios. We are sad to report that Elliot ran out into the street, was run over by a car before *Three in a Cage* was finished. The sadness of his death was too immediate to put into this book. We miss his presence and the princely air he lent to all of us at Aztec Studios.

Life is full of compromises. I have agreed to make new patterns in soft colors that would enhance homes north of the border, as well as make some geometric designs. I have agreed (for the time being) to limit our prehispanic tapestries to the beauty of the Maya Royalty. In exchange, Max and Francisco have agreed to not fear the mystique of our present weavings, to do the dishes and other chores without being asked, and to take on more responsibility for the gallery.

Francisco and Max and I are happy to greet visitors interested in seeing our weavings, even those who ring the doorbell when we are not open... if they are prepared to catch me writing my next book in my old snowflake robe.

Peace and Feathers, Janice Kimball

About the Author

The second half of Janice Kimball's six lives began after she had reached a stable platform following a life that had been fear-filled and desolate. She had by then worked her way up to a nine on the civil service exam ladder but found herself in a program she did not believe in, leading a life that had nothing to do with who she was. She was weary of 'passing' in her world of educated people and wanted to rid herself of that fraudulent feeling that maybe all junior high school drop outs have if they have achieved some measure of success.

Janice married her second husband, an actor, and moved from her hometown of Detroit to Chicago with him. She worked her way through undergraduate school as an assistant instructor in the art department teaching generative art and visual books, receiving her Bachelor of Fine Arts with a minor in writing from *Columbia College, Chicago*. She went on to complete her formal studies at the *University of Illinois* in their studio arts program as a painter. She graduated with a Master in Fine Arts at the age of fifty, followed by a divorce. During this time Janice was exhibiting her work in several Chicago galleries, and her art is in the permanent collections at the *Ukranium Museum of Contemporary Art* and *Columbia College, Chicago*, as well as *Henry Ford Community College* in Detroit.

Returning to Detroit, Janice bought a gutted Victorian home on the historical register in Detroit's inner city. She opened her studio there while restoring it, an eight-year project. She was employed as adjunct faculty at *Marygrove College*, *Wayne County Community College*, and *Henry Ford Community College* simultaneously for the first four years, then accepted a tenured position for *Detroit Public Schools* teaching in the inner city where she earned enough money to complete, with the help of her brother Kurt, the restoration of her Victorian home. Finished, it was on the *Detroit Institute of Art Founders Society* annual home tour filled with her art.

As a teacher at *Pershing High School* in Detroit, Janice never became accustomed to reading her students faces, mostly innocent faces wanting to receive hope, faces that mirrored a life lived in fear. In a foolish moment Janice 'took on' a gang leader who had intimidated her class. She was assaulted by his followers in the hallway after school and suffered a head injury after which she was no longer able to cope. After a Workmen's Compensation settlement, Janice sold her beloved home, only knowing that her stay in Detroit was up.

It had been just hours after a whirlwind of goodbyes that Janice's plane landed in the Guadalajara.. She stood in the taxi line with her companion, Construction Cat, cradled in his carrier clutched to her breast, three suitcases beside her containing her favorite pillow, cat food, bug spray, a bottle of purified water, a roll of canvas, a fistful of brushes, paint, hair conditioner, M and M's, and other necessities. She handed the driver a paper that said 'Ajijic,' a Mexican village where she knew nobody, and she was on her way to a new life, all encumbrances burned behind her.

After a few years of recuperation Janice again became 'alive,' opening *The Kimball Gallery* in Chapala in 2000 to foster communication between Lake Chapala's expatriate art community and local Mexican artists. Since then Janice has been honored as a Mexican artist by the *National Camera de Commercial* in Guadalajara, had a one man exhibition in the prestigious *'El Refugio'* in Tlaquepaque and at the *Ajijic Cultural Center* in addition to *Gallery Efren Gonzales*, and in her own gallery. After becoming partners with weaver Teo Urzúa she opened *Kimball-Urzúa Art* and Weaving Studios in central Ajijic while building *Aztec Art and Weaving Studios*, the live/work, art, and living space where she lives with Francisco Urzúa Inés and Max Bird today.

In 2009 a major shift occurred in Janice's life when the man that had stalked her for the first twenty five years of her adult life died. She was overwhelmed by her relief and no longer felt the constraint of expressing herself in only a visual way. She began to write…and write. She wrote about who she was, where she was, what she was, in a freedom of pure exposure. *Three in a Cage* is a result of that creative freedom. Since 2009 Janice has also written for the *Ojo del Lago, Lake Chapala Review, and Mexico Insights* online magazine, Mexico's leading English language publications. She has a monthly column, Art Talk in the *Lake Chapala Review* which began in 2009.

Janice does not know if she will ever write about her first three lives. Her next book is a collection of short stories set in Mexico. She says that maybe it is enough to know that she can now write whatever she wants without the fear of it inciting a new interest in her stalker.

Janice reserves Thursdays for designing tapestries for Francisco and for greeting those who come to see their weavings and the paintings and collages that remain from Janice's life as an artist. Francisco takes the helm with Max

176

Bird and opens the gallery Fridays, (and on other days at his whim). Their Gallery, one mile west of Ajijic, is facing Janice's Rancho del Oro Serpent Mural on the main highway.

Aztec Art and Weaving Studios
232 Carretera Poniente, lake side
Rancho del Oro, West Ajijic,
Jalisco, Mexico 45920

www.janicekimball.com
janicekimballmx@gmail.com
www.facebook.com/janicekimballmx

Acknowledgements

I want to thank my dear friend Suzanna Baillergeau, and Judy King, the editor of the *Lake Chapala Review* and *Mexico Insights* on-line magazine for believing in me and encouraging me in my original quest to become a writer.

This book is richer because of the whole hearted critique and editing of distinguished poet and columnist Jim Tipton and writer Patricia Hemingway. I cannot imagine bringing it to completion without them. I also deeply thank all of the members of my Chapala writers group, the Ajijic writers group and its originator and captain, Alejandro Grattan, author of *Dark Side of the Dream* and editor of the *Ojo del Lago*, and especially Victoria Schmidt, Herbert Piekow, Jeremy Monroe, and poet, Margaret Van Every, as well as the members of my monthly writers salon who have generously supported this book and have given me excellent suggestions as they walked along with me in the process of writing it.

I also want to acknowledge and thank authors Kelly Hayes-Raitt, Dr. Roberto Moulon and Robert Drynen for their great advice, Betty Wright, for her problem solving when she takes the helm of the computer, and my brother, Kurt Norris, without whose help I might not be in Mexico's heartland, and last but not least, my trusty companions, Francisco Urzúa Inés and Max Bird…and Teo Urzúa for still being friends with me.

That's all for now folks! Do stop by.

Made in the USA
Lexington, KY
28 November 2012